WHEN MAGGIE NEELY'S BROTHER goes missing, she's determined to find him. But she never suspects that the trail will lead her into the most secret heart of the Night World, a kingdom where no outsider has stepped in five hundred years.

The kingdom is ruled by the young vampire prince Delos . . . who keeps all humans as slaves. When Delos falls in love with Maggie, he frees her and demands that she join him in his life of dark pleasure. He's handsome, he's romantic—Maggie can hardly resist him. But did he kill Maggie's brother? And who are the strange people searching the kingdom for a Wild Power? Maggie won't give up until she learns the truth—even if it means destroying Delos and his secret land. If he doesn't destroy her first. . . .

THE NIGHT WORLD
SERIES

· · · · · · · · · · · · · · · · · · ·

NIGHT WORLD · BOOK EIGHT

BLACK DAWN

L. J. SMITH

SIMON PULSE

NEW YORK   LONDON   TORONTO   SYDNEY   NEW DELHI

SIMON PULSE

An imprint of Simon & Schuster Children's Publishing Division

1230 Avenue of the Americas, New York, New York 10020

This Simon Pulse hardcover edition August 2017

Text copyright © 1997 by Lisa J. Smith

Cover illustration copyright © 2017 by Neal Williams

Endpaper art of flowers, heart, and sunburst respectively copyright © 2017 by Liliya Shlapak, Nattle, and Ezepov Dmitry/Shutterstock.com

Endpaper art of ornamental flourishes copyright © 2017 by Thinkstock

All rights reserved, including the right of reproduction in whole or in part in any form.

SIMON PULSE and colophon are registered trademarks of Simon & Schuster, Inc.

NIGHT WORLD is a trademark of Lisa J. Smith

For information about special discounts for bulk purchases, please contact Simon & Schuster Special Sales at 1-866-506-1949 or business@simonandschuster.com.

The Simon & Schuster Speakers Bureau can bring authors to your live event.

For more information or to book an event contact the Simon & Schuster Speakers Bureau at 1-866-248-3049 or visit our website at www.simonspeakers.com.

Cover designed by Regina Flath

Interior designed by Mike Rosamilia

The text of this book was set in Adobe Garamond.

Manufactured in the United States of America

2 4 6 8 10 9 7 5 3 1

Library of Congress Control Number 2016948196

ISBN 978-1-4814-9818-0 (hc)

ISBN 978-1-4814-9819-7 (eBook)

For Michael Penny
and Matthew Penny

CHAPTER 1

Maggie Neely woke up to the sound of her mother screaming.

She'd gone to bed as usual, with Jake the Great Dane sprawled heavily across her feet and the three cats jockeying for position around her head. Her cheek was resting on her open geometry book; there were homework papers scattered among the blankets, along with fragments of potato chips and an empty bag. She was wearing her jeans and a flowered pajama top plus the only two socks she'd been able to find last night: one red velveteen anklet and one blue cotton slouch sock.

Those particular socks would eventually mean the difference between life and death for her, but at the moment Maggie had no idea of that.

She was simply startled and disoriented from being wakened suddenly. She'd never heard this kind of screaming before, and she wondered how she could be so certain it was her mother doing it.

Something . . . really bad is happening, Maggie realized slowly. The worst.

The clock on her nightstand said 2:11 a.m.

And then before she even realized she was moving, she was lurching across her bedroom floor, with piles of dirty clothes and sports equipment trying to trip her up. She banged her shin on a wastebasket in the middle of the room and plowed right on through. The hallway was dim, but the living room at the end was blazing with light and the screams were coming from there.

Jake trotted along beside her. When they got to the foyer by the living room he gave a half growl, half bark.

Maggie took in the whole scene in a glance. It was one of those moments when everything changes forever.

The front door was open, letting in the cold air of a November night in Washington. Maggie's father was wearing a short bathrobe and holding her mother, who was pulling and tearing at him as if she were trying to get away, screaming breathlessly all the while. And in the doorway four people were standing: two sheriffs, a National Park ranger, and Sylvia Weald.

Sylvia. Her brother Miles's girlfriend.

And knowledge hit her quick and hard as a hammer blow.

My brother is dead, Maggie thought.

CHAPTER 2

Beside her, Jake growled again, but Maggie only heard it distantly. No one else even looked toward them.

I can't believe how well I'm taking this, Maggie thought. Something's wrong with me. I'm not hysterical at all.

Her mind had gotten hold of the idea quite clearly, but there was no reaction in her body, no terrible feeling in her stomach. An instant later it swept over her, exactly what she'd been afraid of. A wash of adrenaline that made her skin tingle painfully and a horrible sensation of falling in her stomach. A numbness that started in her cheeks and spread to her lips and jaw.

Oh, please, she thought stupidly. Please let it not be true. Maybe he's just hurt. That would be all right. He had an accident and he's hurt—but not dead.

But if he were hurt her mother wouldn't be standing there screaming. She would be on her way to the hospital, and nobody could stop her. So that didn't work, and Maggie's mind, darting and wheeling like a frightened little animal, had to go back to *Please don't let this be true.*

Strangely, at that moment, it seemed as if there might be some way to make it not true. If she turned around and sneaked back to her bedroom before anyone saw her; if she got into bed and pulled the blankets over her head and shut her eyes . . .

But she couldn't leave her mother screaming like this.

Just then the screams died down a little. Her father was speaking in a voice that didn't sound at all like his voice. It was a sort of choked whisper. "But why didn't you tell us you were going climbing? If you left on Halloween then it's been six days. We didn't even know our son was missing. . . ."

"I'm sorry." Sylvia was whispering, too. "We didn't expect to be gone long. Miles's roommates knew we were going, but nobody else. It was just a spur-of-the-moment thing—we didn't have classes on Halloween and the weather was so nice and Miles said, hey, let's go out to Chimney Rock. And we just *went. . . ."*

Hey, let's go. He used to say that kind of thing to me, Maggie thought with a strange, dazed twinge. But not since he met Sylvia.

The male sheriff was looking at Maggie's father. "You weren't surprised that you hadn't heard from your son since last Friday?"

"No. He's gotten so independent since he moved out to

go to college. One of his roommates called this afternoon to ask if Miles was here—but he didn't say that Miles had been gone for almost a week. I just thought he'd missed a class or something. . . ." Maggie's father's voice trailed off.

The sheriff nodded. "Apparently his roommates thought he'd taken a little unauthorized vacation," he said. "They got worried enough to call us tonight—but by then a ranger had already picked up Sylvia."

Sylvia was crying. She was tall but willowy, fragile-looking. Delicate. She had shimmering hair so pale it was almost silvery and clear eyes the exact color of wood violets. Maggie, who was short and round-faced, with fox-colored hair and brown eyes, had always envied her.

But not now. Nobody could look at Sylvia now without feeling pity.

"It happened that first evening. We started up, but then the weather started turning bad and we turned around. We were moving pretty fast." Sylvia stopped and pressed a fist against her mouth.

"It's kind of a risky time of year for climbing," the female sheriff began gently, but Sylvia shook her head.

And she was right, Maggie thought. It wasn't that bad. Sure, it rained here most of the fall, but sometimes what the weather people called a high pressure cell settled in and the skies stayed blue for a month. All hikers knew that.

Besides, Miles wasn't scared of weather. He was only

eighteen but he'd done lots of hard climbs in Washington's Olympic and Cascade ranges. He'd keep climbing all winter, getting alpine experience in snow and storms.

Sylvia was going on, her voice getting more jerky and breathless. "Miles was . . . he'd had the flu a week before and he wasn't completely over it. But he seemed okay, strong. It happened when we were rappelling down. He was laughing and joking and everything. . . . I never thought he might be tired enough to make a mistake. . . ." Her voice wavered and turned into a ragged sob and the ranger put his arm around her.

Something inside Maggie froze. A mistake? Miles?

She was prepared to hear about a sudden avalanche or a piece of equipment failing. Even Sylvia falling and knocking Miles off. But Miles making a mistake?

Maggie stared at Sylvia, and suddenly something in the pitiful figure bothered her.

There was something odd about that delicately flushed face and those tear-drenched violet eyes. It was all too perfect, too tragic, as if Sylvia were an Academy Award–winning actress doing a famous scene—and enjoying it.

"I don't know *how* it happened," Sylvia was whispering. "The anchor was good. We should have had a backup anchor, but we were in a hurry. And he must have . . . oh, God, there must have been something wrong with his harness. Maybe the buckle wasn't fastened right, or the carabiners might have been upside down. . . ."

No.

Suddenly Maggie's feelings crystalized. It was as if everything came into focus at once.

That's impossible. That's *wrong.*

Miles was too good. Smart and strong and an amazing technical climber. Confident but careful. Maggie only hoped she'd be that good someday.

No way he'd buckle his harness wrong, or clip his 'biners upside down. No matter how sick he was. In fact, no way he'd go without a backup anchor. *I'm* the one who tries to do things like that, and then he yells at me that if I'm not careful I'm going to have an adventure.

Miles doesn't.

So it meant Sylvia was lying.

The thought came to Maggie on a little wave of shock. It made her feel as if she were suddenly speeding backward, or as if the room were receding from her very fast.

But *why*? Why would Sylvia make up such a terrible story? It didn't make any sense.

Sylvia had a hand half covering her eyes now.

"I looked for him, but . . . there was icefall . . . a crevasse . . ."

No body. She's saying there's *no body.*

With that, a new wave of heat swept over Maggie. And, strangely, what made her certain of it was Sylvia's eyes.

Those violet eyes had been turned down for most of the time Sylvia had been talking, fixed on the Spanish tiles in the entry hall. But now, as Sylvia got to the last revelation, they had shifted toward Maggie. Toward Maggie's feet. They fixed there, slid away, and then came back and stayed.

It made Maggie glance down at her own feet.

My socks. She's staring at my socks.

One red and one blue—and she's noticing that. Like an actress who's said the same lines often enough that she doesn't even need to pay attention to them anymore.

All at once, hot anger was burning through Maggie's shock, filling her so there was no room for anything else. She stared hard at Sylvia, who seemed to be very far away but very bright. And in that same instant she knew for certain.

This girl is lying.

She must have done something—something terrible. And she can't show us Miles's body—or maybe there isn't a body because he's still alive.

Yes! Maggie felt suddenly lifted by hope. It *is* all a mistake. There's no reason for Miles to be dead. All we have to do is make Sylvia tell the truth.

But nobody else in the room knew. They were all listening as Sylvia went on with her story. They all believed.

"I didn't get out before the weather hit. . . . I had to stay in the tent for three days. When I got out I was so weak, but I managed to signal to some climbers. They saved me, took care of me. . . . By then it was too late to look for him. I knew there was no chance he'd made it through that storm. . . ."

She broke down completely.

The ranger began talking about weather conditions and recovery efforts, and suddenly Maggie's mother was making strange gasping noises and sinking toward the floor.

"Mom!" Frightened, Maggie started toward her. Her father looked up and seemed to realize for the first time that she was there.

"Oh, Maggie. We've had some bad news."

He's trying to take care of me. But he doesn't realize . . . I've got to tell him. . . .

"Dad," she said urgently. "Listen. There's something—"

"Maggie," her mother interrupted, stretching out a hand. She sounded rational, but there was something wild in her eyes. "I'm so sorry, baby. Something awful has happened—"

And then she fainted. Suddenly Maggie's father was staggering under dead weight. And then the ranger and one of the sheriffs were brushing past Maggie. They were holding her mother up, and her mother's head was *lolling*, moving around on a boneless neck, and her mother's mouth and eyes were part open and part closed. A new kind of awful feeling came to Maggie, making her weak and giddy. She was afraid she would faint herself.

"Where can we—" the male officer began.

"There's the couch," Maggie's father said hoarsely at the same time. There was no room for Maggie. She could only stand out of the way and dizzily watch them carry her mother.

As they did, Sylvia began murmuring. It took Maggie a moment to focus on the words. "I'm so sorry. I'm so sorry. I wish there was something . . . I should go home now."

"You stay right here," the female officer said, looking toward Maggie's mother. "You're in no condition to be walking anywhere. You'd be in the hospital now if you hadn't insisted on coming here first."

"I don't need a hospital. I'm just so tired. . . ."

The officer turned. "Why don't you go sit in the car?" she said gently.

Sylvia nodded. She looked fragile and sad as she walked down the path toward the squad car. It was a beautiful exit, Maggie thought. You could practically hear the theme music swelling.

But Maggie was the only one with the chance to appreciate it. She was the only one watching as Sylvia reached the car . . . and paused.

And then turned away from it and continued on down the street.

And the end credits run, Maggie thought.

Then she thought, She's going to her apartment.

Maggie stood frozen, pulled in two directions.

She wanted to stay and help her mother. But something inside her was utterly furious and focused and it was screaming at her to follow Sylvia.

Instinct had always been Maggie's strong point.

She hung there for a moment, with her heart pounding so hard that it seemed to be coming out of her mouth. Then she ducked her head and clenched her fists.

It was a gesture the girls on her soccer team would have recognized. It meant that Steely Neely had made up her mind and was going to rush in where smarter people feared to tread. Look out, world; it's stomping time.

Maggie whirled and dashed back down the hall into her bedroom.

She slapped the light switch on and looked around as if she'd never seen the place before. What did she need—and why did she always keep it so messy? How could she *find* things?

She kicked and pulled at a pile of bath towels until a pair of high-top tennis shoes emerged, then she jammed her feet in them. There was no time to change her pajama top. She snatched a dark blue jacket off the floor and found herself, just for a moment, nose to nose with a photograph stuck into the frame of her mirror.

A picture of Miles, on the summit of Mount Rainier. He was grinning and giving the thumbs-up sign. His hat was off and his auburn hair was shining in the sun like red gold. He looked handsome and a little wicked.

Scrawled in black marker across white snow was "For the bossiest, nosiest, stubbornest, BEST little sister in the world. Love, Miles."

With no idea *why* she was doing it, Maggie pulled the

picture out of the mirror. She shoved it in her jacket pocket and ran back down the hall.

Everyone was gathered around the couch now. Even Jake was nosing his way in. Maggie couldn't see her mother, but the lack of frantic activity told her that there wasn't any crisis going on. Everyone seemed quiet and restrained.

It'll just take a few minutes. It's better for me not to tell them anything until I'm sure. I'll probably be back before they even realize I'm gone.

With that jumble of excuses in her mind, she slipped out the front door to follow Sylvia.

CHAPTER 3

I t was raining, of course. Not a terrible storm, just a steady spitting patter that Maggie hardly noticed. It plastered her hair down but it also concealed the noise of her steps.

And the low-lying clouds blocked out Mount Rainier. In clear weather the mountain loomed over the city like an avenging white angel.

I'm actually following somebody, Maggie thought. She could hardly believe it, but she was really moving down her own home street like a spy, skirting cars and ducking behind rhododendron bushes.

While all the time keeping her eyes on the slender figure in front of her.

That was what kept her going. She might have felt silly and almost embarrassed to be doing this—but not tonight. What had happened put her far beyond embarrassment, and if she started to relax inside and feel the faint pricklings of uncertainty, memory surged up again and swept everything else away.

The memory of Sylvia's voice. *The buckle might not have been fastened right.* And the memory of her mother's hand going limp as her body sagged.

I'll follow you no matter where you go, Maggie thought. And then . . .

She didn't know what then. She was trusting to instinct, letting it guide her. It was stronger and smarter than she was at the moment.

Sylvia's apartment was in the U district, the college area around the University of Washington. It was a long walk, and by the time they reached it, the rain was coming down harder. Maggie was glad to get out of it and follow Sylvia into the underground garage.

This is a dangerous place, she thought as she walked into the echoing darkness. But it was simply a note made by her mind, with no emotion attached. At the moment she felt as if she could punch a mugger hard enough to splatter him against the wall.

She kept a safe distance as Sylvia waited for the elevator, then headed for the stairs. Third floor. Maggie trotted up faster than the elevator could make it and arrived not even breathing hard. The door of the stairwell was half open and she watched from behind it as Sylvia walked to an apartment door and raised a hand to knock.

Before she could, the door opened. A boy who looked a little older than Maggie was holding it, letting a couple of laughing girls out. Music drifted to Maggie, and the smell of incense.

They're having a party in there.

That shouldn't be so shocking—it was Saturday night. Sylvia lived with three roommates; *they* were undoubtedly the ones having the party. But as the girls walked past Sylvia they smiled and nodded and Sylvia smiled and nodded back before walking calmly through the door.

Hardly the sort of thing you do when your boyfriend's just been killed, Maggie thought fiercely. And it doesn't exactly fit the "tragic heroine" act, either.

Then she noticed something. When the boy holding the door let go, it had swung almost shut—but not quite.

Can I do it? Maybe. If I look confident. I'd have to walk right in as if I belonged, not hesitate.

And hope she doesn't notice. Then get behind her. See if she talks to anybody, what she says . . .

The laughing girls had caught the elevator. Maggie walked straight up to the door and, without pausing, she pushed it open and went inside.

Look confident, she thought, and she kept on going, instinctively moving toward a side wall. Her entry didn't seem to have caused a stir, and it was easier than she'd thought to walk in among these strangers. The apartment was very dark, for one thing. And the music was medium loud, and everybody seemed to be talking.

The only problem was that she couldn't see Sylvia. She put her back to the wall and waited for her eyes to adjust.

Not over there—not by the stereo. Probably in one of the bedrooms in back, changing.

It was as she moved toward the little hallway that led to the bedrooms that Maggie really noticed the strangeness. Something about this apartment, about this party . . . was off. Weird. It gave her the same feeling that Sylvia did.

Danger.

This place is dangerous.

Everybody there was so good-looking—or else ugly in a really fashionable way, as if they'd just stepped off MTV. But there was an air about them that reminded Maggie of the sharks at the Seattle Aquarium. A coldness that couldn't be seen, only sensed.

There is something so wrong here. Are they all drug dealers or something? Satanists? Some kind of junior mafia? They just feel so *evil.* . . .

Maggie herself felt like a cat with all its fur standing on end.

When she heard a girl's voice coming from the first bedroom, she froze, hoping it was Sylvia.

"Really, the most secret place you've ever imagined." It wasn't Sylvia. Maggie could just see the speaker through the crack in the door. She was pale and beautiful, with one long black braid, and she was leaning forward and lightly touching the back of a boy's hand.

"So exotic, so mysterious—it's a place from the past, you see. It's ancient, and everybody's forgotten about it, but it's still there. Of course, it's terribly dangerous—but not for *us*. . . ."

Not relevant, Maggie's mind decided, and she stopped listening. Somebody's weird vacation plans; nothing to do with Sylvia or Miles.

She kept on edging down the hall. The door at the end was shut.

Sylvia's bedroom.

Well, she has to be in there; she isn't anywhere else.

With a surreptitious glance behind her, Maggie crept closer to the door. She leaned toward it until her cheek touched the cool white paint on the wood, all the while straining her eyes toward the living room in case somebody should turn her way. She held her breath and tried to look casual, but her heart was beating so loudly that she could only hear it and the music.

Certainly there was nobody talking behind the door. Maggie's hopes of eavesdropping faded.

All right, then, I'll go in. And there's no point in trying to be stealthy; she's going to *notice*.

So I'll just do it.

It helped that she was so keyed up. She didn't even need to brace herself; her body was at maximum tension already. Despite her sense that there was something menacing about this whole place, she wasn't frightened, or at least not in a way that *felt* like fear. It felt like rage instead, like being desperately ready for battle. She wanted to grab something and shake it to pieces.

She took hold of the knob and pushed the door open.

A new smell of incense hit her as the air rushed out. It was stronger than the living room smell, more earthy and musky, with an overlying sweetness that Maggie didn't like. The bedroom was even darker than the hall, but Maggie stepped inside. There was tension on the door somehow; as soon as she let go of it, it whispered shut behind her.

Sylvia was standing beside the desk.

She was alone, and she was still wearing the Gore-Tex climbing outfit she'd had on at Maggie's house. Her shimmering fine hair was starting to dry and lifting up like little angel feathers away from her forehead.

She was doing something with a brass incense burner, adding pinches of powder and what looked like herbs to it. That was where the sickeningly sweet smell was coming from.

Maggie had planned—as far as she'd planned anything at all—to rush right up and get in Sylvia's face. To startle her into some kind of confession. She was going to say, "I need to talk to you." But before she could get the first word out, Sylvia spoke without looking up.

"What a shame. You really should have stayed home with your parents, you know." Her voice was cool and languorous, not hasty and certainly not regretful.

Maggie stopped in her tracks.

Now, what's *that* supposed to mean? Is it a threat? Fine. Whatever. I can threaten, too.

But she was taken by surprise, and she had to swallow hard before speaking roughly. "I don't know what you're talking about, but at least you've dropped the weepy-weepy act. You were really bad at it."

"I thought I was very good," Sylvia said and added a pinch of something to the incense burner. "I'm sure the officers thought so, too."

Once again, Maggie was startled. This wasn't going at all as she expected. Sylvia was so calm, so much at ease. So much in control of the situation.

Not anymore, Maggie thought.

She just *admitted* it was an act. All that chokey stuff while she was talking about Miles . . .

Fury uncoiled in Maggie's stomach like a snake.

She took three fast steps forward. "You know why I'm here. I want to know what really happened to my brother."

"I told you—"

"You told a bunch of lies! I don't know what the truth is. The only thing I *do* know is that Miles would never make a stupid mistake like not buckling his harness. Look, if *you* did something dumb—if he's lying out there hurt or something, and you were too scared to admit it—you'd better tell me right now." It was the first time she'd put into words a reason for Sylvia to be lying.

Sylvia looked up.

Maggie was startled. In the light of the single candle by the incense burner, Sylvia's eyes were not violet but a more reddish color, like amethyst. They were large and clear and the light seemed to play in them, quivering.

"Is that what you think happened?" Sylvia asked softly.

"I said, I don't *know* what happened!" Maggie felt dizzy suddenly, and fought it, glaring into Sylvia's strange eyes. "Maybe you had a fight or something. Maybe you've got some other boyfriend. Maybe you weren't even out climbing on Halloween in the first place. All I know is that you lied and that there's no body to find. And I want to know the truth!"

Sylvia looked back steadily, the candlelight dancing in her purple eyes. "You know what your brother told me about you?" she asked musingly. "Two things. The first was that you never gave up. He said, 'Maggie's no rocket scientist, but once she gets hold of something she's just like a little bull terrier.' And the second was that you were a complete sucker for anybody in trouble. A real bleeding heart."

She added a few fingernail-sized chips of smooth bark to the mixture that was smoking in the incense burner.

"Which is too bad," she went on thoughtfully. "Strong-willed and compassionate: that's a real recipe for disaster."

Maggie had had it.

"What happened to Miles? What did you *do* to him?"

Sylvia laughed, a little secret laugh. "I'm afraid you couldn't guess if you spent the rest of your short life trying." She shook her head. "It was too bad, actually. I liked him. We could have been good together."

Maggie wanted to know one thing. "Is he dead?"

"I told you, you'll never find out. Not even when you go where you're going."

Maggie stared at her, trying to make sense of this. She couldn't. When she spoke it was in a level voice, staring into Sylvia's eyes.

"I don't know what your problem is—maybe you're crazy or something. But I'm telling you right now, if you've done anything to my brother, I am going to *kill* you."

She'd never said anything like this before, but now it came out quite naturally, with force and conviction. She was so angry that all she could see was Sylvia's face. Her stomach was knotted and she actually felt a burning in her middle, as if there were a glowing fire there.

"Now," she said, "*are you going to tell me what happened to him?*"

Sylvia sighed, spoke quietly. "No."

Before Maggie quite knew she was doing it, she had reached out and grabbed the front of Sylvia's green Gore-Tex jacket with both hands.

Something sparked in Sylvia's eyes. For a moment, she looked startled and interested and grudgingly respectful. Then she sighed again, smiling faintly.

"And now you're going to kill me?"

"Listen, you . . ." Maggie leaned in. She stopped.

"Listen to what?"

Maggie blinked. Her eyes were stinging suddenly. The smoke from the incense burner was rising directly into her face.

"You . . ."

I feel strange, Maggie thought.

Very strange. Dizzy. It seemed to come over her all at once. There was a pattern of flashing gray spreading across her vision. Her stomach heaved and she felt a wave of queasiness.

"Having a problem?" Sylvia's voice seemed to come from far away.

The incense.

It was rising right in her face. And now . . .

"What did you do to me?" Maggie gasped. She reeled backward, away from the smoke, but it was too late. Her knees were horribly rubbery. Her body seemed to be far away somehow, and the sparkling pattern blinded her completely.

She felt the back of her legs come up against a bed. Then they simply weren't supporting her anymore; she was slithering down, unable to catch herself with her useless arms. Her lips were numb.

"You know, for a moment there, I thought I might be in trouble," Sylvia's voice was saying calmly. "But I was wrong. The truth is that you're just an ordinary girl, after all. Weak and powerless—and ordinary. How could you even think about going up against me? Against my people?"

Am I dying? Maggie wondered. I'm losing myself. I can't see and I can't move. . . .

"How could you come here and attack me? How could you think you had a chance at winning?" Even Sylvia's voice seemed to be getting more and more distant. "You're pathetic. But now you'll find out what happens when you mess with real power. You'll learn. . . ."

The voice was gone. There was only a rushing noise in an endless blackness.

Miles, Maggie thought. I'm sorry. . . .

Then she stopped thinking at all.

CHAPTER 4

Maggie was dreaming. She knew she was dreaming, and that was strange enough, but what was even stranger was the fact that she knew it wasn't an ordinary dream.

This was something . . . that came from outside her, that was being . . . *sent.* Some deep part of her mind fumbled for the proper words, seething with frustration, even while the normal part of her was busy staring around her and being afraid.

Mist. Mist everywhere, white tendrils that snaked gracefully across her vision and coiled around her like genii that had just been let out of lamps. She had the feeling that there were dark shapes out in the mist; she seemed to see them looming out of the corner of her eye, but as soon as she turned they were obscured again.

Gooseflesh rose on Maggie's arms. It wasn't just the touch of the mist. There was a noise that made the hairs on the back

of her neck tingle. It was just at the threshold of hearing, distorted by distance or something else, and it seemed to be calling over and over again, "Who are you?"

Give me a *break*, Maggie thought. She shook her head hard to get rid of the prickly feeling on her neck. This is just way too . . . too *Gothic*. Do I always have corny dreams like this?

But the next moment something happened that sent a new chill washing over her, this time one of simple, everyday alarm. Something was coming through the mist, fast.

She turned, stiffening. And then, strangely, everything seemed to change at once.

The mist began to recede. She saw a figure, dark against it, nothing more than a silhouette at first. For just an instant she thought of Miles—but the thought was gone almost as quickly as it came. It was a boy, but a stranger, she could tell by the shape of him and the way he moved. He was breathing hard and calling in a desperate voice, "Where are you? Where are you?"

So that was it. Not "*Who* are you," Maggie thought.

"Where are you? Maggie! Where are you?"

The sound of her own name startled her. But even as she drew in a sharp breath, he turned and saw her.

And stopped short. The mist was almost gone now and she could see his face. His expression was one of wonder and relief and joy.

"Maggie," he whispered.

Maggie stood rooted to the spot. She didn't know him. She

was positive she had never seen him before. But he was staring at her as if . . . as if she were the most important thing in the universe to him, and he'd been searching for her for years until he'd almost given up hope. She was too astonished to move as he suddenly erupted from stillness. In three long steps he was in front of her, his hands closing on her shoulders.

Gently. Not possessively. But as if he had the absolute right to do this, and as if he needed to convince himself she was real.

"It worked. I got through," he said.

He was the most striking person she'd ever seen. Dark hair, a little rough and tousled, with a tendency to wave. Smooth fair skin, elegant bones. A mouth that looked as if it normally might be proud and willful, but right now was simply vulnerable.

And fearless, brilliant yellow eyes.

It was those eyes that held her, arresting and startling in an already distinctive face. No, she had never seen him before. She would have remembered.

He was a whole head taller than she was, and lithe and nicely muscled. But Maggie didn't have a feeling of being overpowered. There was so much tender anxiety in his face, and something near pleading in those fierce, black-lashed golden eyes.

"Listen, I know you don't understand, and I'm sorry. But it was so hard getting through—and there isn't much time."

Dazed and bewildered, Maggie latched onto the last sentence almost mechanically. "What do you mean—getting through?"

"Never mind. Maggie, you have to leave; do you understand that? As soon as you wake up, you get out of here."

"Leave *where?*" Maggie was more confused than ever, not for lack of information, but because she was suddenly threatened by too much of it. She needed to remember—where had she gone to sleep? Something had happened, something involving Miles. She'd been worried about him. . . .

"My brother," she said with sudden urgency. "I was looking for my brother. I need to find him." Even though she couldn't remember exactly why.

The golden eyes clouded over. "You can't think about him now. I'm sorry."

"You know something a—"

"Maggie, the important thing is for you to get away safe. And to do that you have to go as soon as you wake up. I'm going to show you the way."

He pointed through the mist, and suddenly Maggie could see a landscape, distant but clear, like a film being projected on a veil of smoke.

"There's a pass, just below the big overhanging rock. Do you see it?"

Maggie didn't understand why she *needed* to see it. She didn't recognize the landscape, although it might have been anywhere in the Olympics or the Cascade mountain range above the tree line.

"First you find the place where you see three peaks together, the same height and leaning toward each other. Do you see? And then you look down until you find the overhanging rock. It's shaped like a wave breaking. Do you see?"

His voice was so urgent and imperious that Maggie had to answer. "I see. But—"

"Remember it. Find it. Go and never look back. If you get away all right, the rest doesn't matter." His face was pale now, the features carved in ice, "The whole world can fall into ruin, for all I care."

And then, with the suddenness that characterized all his movements, he leaned forward and kissed her.

A nice kiss, on the cheek. She felt his warm, quick breath there, then his lips pressing lightly, and then a sudden quivering in them, as if he were overcome by some strong emotion. Passion, maybe, or excruciating sadness.

"I love you," he whispered, his breath stirring the hair by her ear. "I did love you. Always remember that."

Maggie was dizzy with confusion. She didn't understand anything, and she should push this stranger away. But she didn't *want* to. However frightened she was, it wasn't of him. In fact, she had an irresistible feeling of peace and security in his arms. A feeling of belonging.

"Who are you?" she whispered.

But before he could answer, everything changed again.

The mist came back. Not slowly, but like fog rolling in, quick and silent, muffling everything. The warm, solid body against Maggie's suddenly seemed insubstantial, as if it were made of fog itself.

"Wait a minute—" She could hear her voice rising in panic, but deadened by the pearly cocoon around her.

And then . . . he was gone. Her arms were holding only emptiness. And all she could see was white.

CHAPTER 5

Maggie woke slowly.

And painfully.

I must be sick, she thought. It was the only explanation for the way she felt. Her body was heavy and achy, her head was throbbing, and her sinuses were completely stuffed up. She was breathing through her mouth, which was so dry and gluey that her tongue stuck to the roof of it.

I was having a dream, she thought. But even as she grasped at bits of it, it dissolved. Something about . . . fog? And a boy.

It seemed vaguely important for her to remember, but even the importance was hard to keep hold of. Besides, another, more practical consideration was overriding it. Thirst. She was dying of thirst.

I need a glass of water. . . .

It took a tremendous effort to lift her head and open her eyes. But when she did, her brain cleared fast. She wasn't in her bedroom. She was in a small, dark, smelly room; a room that was moving jerkily, bouncing her painfully up and down and from side to side. There was a rhythmic noise coming from just outside that she felt she should be able to recognize.

Below her cheek and under her fingers was the roughness of unpainted wood. The ceiling and walls were made of the same silvery, weathered boards.

What kind of room is small and made of wood and . . .

Not a room, she thought suddenly. A *vehicle.* Some kind of wooden cart.

As soon as she realized it, she knew what the rhythmic sound was.

Horses' hooves.

No, it can't be, she thought. It's too bizarre. I *am* sick; I'm probably hallucinating.

But it felt incredibly real for a hallucination. It felt exactly as if she were in a wooden cart being drawn by horses. Over rough ground. Which explained all the jostling.

So what was going *on*? What was she doing here?

Where did I go to sleep?

All at once adrenaline surged through her—and with it a flash of memory. Sylvia. The incense . . .

Miles.

Miles is dead . . . no. He's not. Sylvia said that, but she was lying. And then she said I'd never find out what happened to him. And then she drugged me with that smoke.

It gave Maggie a faint feeling of satisfaction to have put this much together. Even if everything else was completely confusing, she had a solid memory to hang on to.

"You woke up," a voice said. "Finally. This kid says you've been asleep for a day and a half."

Maggie pushed herself up by stages until she could see the speaker. It was a girl with untidy red hair, an angular, intense face, and flat, hard eyes. She seemed to be about Maggie's age. Beside her was a younger girl, maybe nine or ten. She was very pretty, slight, with short blond hair under a red plaid baseball cap. She looked frightened.

"Who are you?" Maggie said indistinctly. Her tongue was thick—she was so *thirsty*. "Where am I? What's going on?"

"Huh. You'll find out," the red-haired girl said.

Maggie looked around. There was a fourth girl in the cart, curled up in the corner with her eyes shut.

Maggie felt stupid and slow, but she tried to gather herself.

"What do you mean I've been asleep for a day and a half?"

The red-haired girl shrugged. "That's what *she* said. I wouldn't know. They just picked me up a few hours ago. I almost made it out of this place, but they caught me."

Maggie stared at her. There was a fresh bruise on one of the girl's angular cheekbones and her lip was swollen.

"What—place?" she said slowly. When nobody answered, she went on, "Look. I'm Maggie Neely. I don't know where this is or what I'm doing here, but the last thing I remember is a girl named Sylvia knocking me out. Sylvia Weald. Do you guys know her?"

The redhead just stared back with narrowed green eyes. The girl lying down didn't stir, and the blond kid in the plaid cap cringed.

"Come on, somebody talk to me!"

"You really don't know what's going on?" the red-haired girl said.

"If I knew, I wouldn't be asking over and over!"

The girl eyed her a moment, then spoke with a kind of malicious pleasure. "You've been sold into slavery. You're a slave now."

Maggie laughed.

It was a short involuntary sound, and it hurt her aching head. The blond kid flinched again. Something in her expression made Maggie's grin fade away.

She felt a cold ripple up her spine.

"Come on," she said. "Give me a break. There aren't slaves anymore!"

"There are here." The redhead smiled again, nastily. "But I bet you don't know where you are, either."

"In Washington State—" Even as she said it, Maggie felt her stomach tighten.

"Wrong. Or right, but it doesn't matter. Technically we may be in Washington, but where we really are is hell."

Maggie was losing her self-control. "What are you *talking* about?"

"Take a look through that crack."

There were lots of cracks in the cart; the pale light that filtered through them was the only illumination. Maggie knelt up and put her eye to a big one, blinking and squinting.

At first she couldn't see much. The cart was bouncing and it was hard to determine what she was looking at. All she knew was that there seemed to be no *color*. Everything was either phosphorescent white or dead black.

Gradually she realized that the white was an overcast sky, and the black was a mountain. A *big* mountain, close enough to smack her face against. It reared up haughtily against the sky, its lower reaches covered with trees that seemed ebony instead of green and swimming with mist. Its top was completely wreathed in clouds; there was no way to judge how high it was.

And beside it was another mountain just like it. Maggie shifted, trying to get a wider view. There were mountains everywhere, in an impenetrable ring surrounding her.

They were . . . scary.

Maggie knew mountains, and loved them, but these were different from any she'd ever seen. So cold, and with that haunted mist creeping everywhere. The place seemed to be full of ghosts, materializing and then disappearing with an almost audible wail.

It was like another world.

Maggie sat down hard, then slowly turned back to look at

the redheaded girl. "Where is this?" she said, and her voice was almost a whisper.

To her surprise, the girl didn't laugh maliciously again. Instead she looked away, with eyes that seemed to focus on some distant and terrible memory, and she spoke in almost a whisper herself. "It's the most secret place in the Night World."

Maggie felt as if the mist outside had reached down the back of her pajama top.

"The *what?*"

"The Night World. It's like an organization. For all of *them*, you know." When Maggie just looked at her, she went on, "Them. The ones that aren't human."

This time what Maggie felt was a plunging in her stomach, and she honestly didn't know if it was because she was locked up in here with a loony, or if some part of her already accepted what the loony was saying. Either way, she was scared sick, and she couldn't say anything.

The girl with red hair flicked a glance at her, and the malicious pleasure came back. "The vampires," she said distinctly, "and the shapeshifters and the witches—"

Oh, God, Maggie thought. *Sylvia.*

Sylvia is a witch.

She didn't know how she knew and probably part of her didn't believe it anyway, but the word was thundering around inside her like an avalanche, gathering evidence as it fell. The incense, those strange purple eyes, the way Miles fell for her so fast and hardly ever called the family after he met her, and changed his whole personality, just as if he'd been under a spell, bewitched and helpless, and, oh, Miles, why didn't I *guess*. . . .

I'm not smart, but I've always been a good judge of character. How could I screw up when it counted?

"They don't normally have places of their own," the red-headed girl was going on; and the words were somehow finding their way to Maggie's ears despite the chaos going on inside her. "Mostly they just live in *our* cities, pretending to be like us. But this valley is special; it's been here in the Cascades for centuries and humans have never found it. It's all surrounded by spells and fog—and those mountains. There's a pass through them, big enough for carts, but only the Night People can see it. It's called the Dark Kingdom."

Oh, *terrific*, Maggie thought numbly. The name was strangely suited to what she'd seen outside. Yellow sunlight was almost impossible to imagine in this place. Those filmy wraiths of mist held it in a shimmering silvery-white spell.

"And you're trying to say that we're all . . . slaves now? But how did you guys get here?"

When the redhead didn't answer, she looked at the little blond girl.

The girl shifted her slight body, gulped. Finally she spoke in a husky little voice.

"I'm P.J. Penobscot. I was—it happened to me on Halloween. I was trick-or-treating." She looked down at herself, and Maggie realized she was wearing a tan cable-knit sweater and a vest. "I was a golfer. And I was only supposed to go on my own block because the weather was getting bad. But my friend Aaron and I went across the street and this car stopped in front of me. . . ." She trailed off and swallowed hard.

Maggie reached over and squeezed her hand. "I bet you were a great golfer."

P.J. smiled wanly. "Thanks." Then her small face hardened and her eyes became distant. "Aaron got away, but this man grabbed me. I tried to hit him with my golf club, but he took it away. He looked at me and then he put me in the car. He was strong."

"He was a professional slave trader," the red-haired girl said. "Both the guys I've seen are pros. That's why they looked at her face—they take pretty slaves when they can get them."

Maggie stared at her, then turned to P.J. "And then what?"

"They put something over my face—I was still fighting and yelling and everything—and then I went to sleep for a while. I woke up in this warehouse place." She breathed once and looked at her thin wrists. "I was chained to a bed and I was all alone. I was alone for a while. And then, maybe it was the next day, they brought in *her*." She nodded at the girl sleeping in the corner.

Maggie looked at the still form. It didn't move except when the cart shook it. "Is she all right?"

"She's sick. They left her there for a long time, maybe

four days, but she never really woke up. I think she's getting worse." P.J.'s voice was quiet and detached. "They came in to give us food, but that was all. And then yesterday they brought *you* in."

Maggie blinked. "To the warehouse."

P.J. nodded solemnly. "You were asleep, too. But I don't know what happened after that. They put the cloth over my face again. When I woke up I was in a van."

"They use those for transport on the other side," the redhaired girl said. "To get up to the pass. Then they switch to a cart. The people in this valley have never seen a car."

"So you mean I slept through all that?" Maggie asked P.J.

P.J. nodded again, and the redhead said, "They probably gave you more of the drug. They try to keep everybody too doped up to fight."

Maggie was chewing her lip. Something had occurred to her. Maybe Sylvia hadn't gone climbing with Miles at all. "So, P.J., you never saw any other slaves besides that girl? You didn't see a boy?" She fished in her jacket pocket and pulled out the photo of Miles. "A boy who looked like this?"

P.J. looked at the photograph gravely, then shook her head. "I never saw him before. He looks like you."

"He's my brother, Miles. He disappeared on Halloween, too. I thought maybe . . ." Maggie shook her head, then held the photograph toward the red-haired girl.

"Never seen him before," the girl said shortly.

Maggie looked at her. For somebody who liked to talk about scary things, she didn't say much that was helpful. "And what about you? How'd you get here?"

The girl snorted. "I told you. I was getting *out* of the valley." Her face tightened. "And I almost made it through the pass, but they caught me and stuck me in here. I should have made them kill me instead."

"Whoa," Maggie said. She glanced at P.J., meaning that they shouldn't frighten her unnecessarily. "It can't be *that* bad."

To her surprise, the girl didn't sneer or get mad. "It's worse," she said, almost whispering again. "Just leave it alone. You'll find out."

Maggie felt the hair at the back of her neck stir. "What are you saying?"

The girl turned, her green eyes burning darkly. "The Night People have to eat," she said. "They can eat normal things, food and water. But the vampires have to drink blood and the shapeshifters have to eat flesh. Is that clear enough for you?"

Maggie sat frozen. She wasn't worried about scaring P.J. anymore. She was too scared herself.

"We're slave labor for them, but we're also a food supply. A food supply that lasts a long time, through lots of feedings," the girl said brusquely.

Maggie ducked her head and clenched her fists. "Well, then, obviously we've got to escape," she said through her teeth.

The redhead gave a laugh so bitter that Maggie felt a chill down her spine.

She looked at P.J. "Do *you* want to escape?"

"Leave her alone!" the redhead snapped. "You don't understand what you're talking about. We're only humans; they're Night People. There's nothing we can do against them, *nothing!*"

"But—"

"Do you know what the Night People do to slaves who try to escape?"

And then the red-haired girl turned her back on Maggie. She did it with a lithe twist that left Maggie startled.

Did I hurt her feelings? Maggie thought stupidly.

The redhead glanced back over her shoulder, at the same time reaching around to grasp the bottom of her shirt in back.

Her expression was unreadable, but suddenly Maggie was nervous.

"What are you doing?"

The red-haired girl gave a strange little smile and pulled the shirt up, exposing her back.

Somebody had been playing tic-tac-toe there.

The lines were cut into the flesh of her back, the scars shiny pink and only half healed. In the squares were x's and o's, raggedy-looking and brighter red because for the most part they'd been burned in. A few looked cut, like the strategic position in the middle which would have been taken first.

Somebody had won, three diagonal *X*s, and had run a burn-line through the winning marks.

Maggie gasped. She kept on gasping. She started to hyperventilate, and then she started to faint.

The world seemed to recede from her, narrowing down to a one-dimensional point of light. But there wasn't room to actually fall over. As she slumped backward, she hit the wall of the cart. The world wobbled and came back, shiny at the edges.

"Oh, God," Maggie said. "Oh, *God*. They did this to you? How could they *do* that?"

"This is nothing," the girl said. "They did it when I escaped the first time. And now I escaped again—and I got caught again. This time they'll do something worse." She let go of her top and it slid down to cover her back again.

Maggie tried to swallow, but her mouth was too dry. Before she knew she was moving, she found herself grabbing the girl's arms from behind.

"What's your name?"

"Who ca—"

"What's your name?"

The red-haired girl gave her a peculiar look over her shoulder. Then her arms lifted slightly under Maggie's hands as she shrugged.

"Jeanne."

"Jeanne. It's got to stop," Maggie said. "We can't let them

do things like that to people. And we've got to get away. If they're already going to punish you for escaping, what difference does it make if you try it again now? Don't you think?"

Maggie liked the way that sounded, calm and competent and logical. The swift decision for action didn't blot out the memory of what she'd just seen, but it made the whole situation more bearable. She'd witnessed an injustice and she was going to do something about it. That simple. Something so wicked had to be fixed, *now.*

She started to cry.

Jeanne turned around, gave her a long, assessing look. P.J. was crying, too, very quietly.

Maggie found her tears running out. They weren't doing any good. When she stopped, Jeanne was still watching her with narrowed eyes.

"So you're going to take on the whole Night World alone," she said.

Maggie wiped her cheeks with her hands. "No, just the ones here."

Jeanne stared at her another moment, then straightened abruptly. "Okay," she said, so suddenly that Maggie was startled. "Let's do it. If we can figure out a way."

Maggie looked toward the back of the cart. "What about those doors?"

"Locked and chained on the outside. It's no good kicking them."

From nowhere, an image came into Maggie's mind. Herself and Miles in a rowboat on Lake Chelan with their grandfather. Deliberately rocking it while their grandfather yelled and fumed.

"What if we all throw our weight from one side to the other? If we could turn the cart over, maybe the doors would pop open. You know how armored cars always seem to do that. Or maybe it would smash one of the walls enough that we could get out."

"And maybe we'd go falling straight down a ravine," Jeanne said acidly. "It's a long way down to the valley, and this road is narrow." But there was a certain unwilling respect in her eyes. "I guess we could try it when we get to a meadow," she said slowly. "I know a place. I'm not saying it would work; it probably won't. But . . ."

"We have to try," Maggie said. She was looking straight at Jeanne. For a moment there was something between them—a flash of understanding and agreement. A bond.

"Once we got out, we'd have to run," Jeanne said, still slowly. "They're sitting up *there*." She pointed to the ceiling at the front of the cart, above Maggie's head. "This thing is like a stagecoach, okay? There's a seat up there, and the two guys are on it. Professional slave traders are tough. They're not going to want us to get away."

"They might get smashed up when we roll over," Maggie said.

Jeanne shook her head sharply. "Night People are strong. It takes a lot more than that to kill them. We'd have to just take off and head for the forest as fast as we could. Our only chance is to get lost in the trees—and hope they can't track us."

"Okay," Maggie said. She looked at P.J. "Do you think you could do that? Just run and keep running?"

P.J. gulped twice, sank her teeth into her top lip, and nodded. She twisted her baseball cap around so the visor faced the back.

"I can run," she said.

Maggie gave her an approving nod. Then she looked at the fourth girl, the one still curled up asleep. She leaned over to touch the girl's shoulder.

"Forget it," Jeanne said shortly. "We can't take her."

Maggie looked up at her, shocked. "What are you talking about? Why not?"

CHAPTER 6

Because there's no point. She's as good as dead already."
Jeanne's expression was as hard and closed as it had
been in the beginning.

"But—"

"Can't you see? She'd slow us down. There's no way she
could run without help. And besides that, P.J. says she's blind."

Blind. A new little shock went though Maggie. What
would that be like, to be in this situation and sick and blind
on top of it?

She tugged on the girl's shoulder gently, trying to see the
averted face.

But she's beautiful.

The girl had smooth skin the color of coffee with cream,
delicate features, high cheekbones, perfect lips. Her black hair
was pulled into a loose, glossy knot on her neck. Her eyes were
shut, long eyelashes trembling as if she were dreaming.

It was more than just the physical features, though. There was a serenity about this girl's face, a gentleness and stillness that was . . . unique.

"Hey, there," Maggie said softly. "Can you hear me? I'm Maggie. What's your name?"

The girl's eyelashes fluttered; her lips parted. To Maggie's surprise, she murmured something. Maggie had to lean down close to catch it

"Arcadia?" she repeated. It was a strange name; she wasn't sure she'd heard right.

The girl seemed to nod, murmuring again.

She can hear me, Maggie thought. She can respond.

"Okay. Can I call you Cady? Listen to me, Cady." Maggie shook the girl's shoulder slightly. "We're in a bad place but we're going to try to escape. If we help you out, do you think you can run?"

Again, the eyelashes fluttered. Then the eyes opened.

Doe eyes, Maggie thought, startled. They were extraordinarily large and clear, a warm brown with an inner radiance. And they might be blind, but Maggie had the oddest sensation that she had just been *seen* more clearly than ever before in her life.

"I'll try," Cady murmured. She sounded dazed and in pain, but quietly rational. "Sometimes I feel strong for a little while." She pushed herself up. Maggie had to help her get into a sitting position.

She's tall. But she's pretty light . . . and I've got good muscles. I can support her.

"What are you *doing*?" Jeanne said in a voice that was not just harsh and impatient but horrified. "Don't you see? You're only making it worse. You should just have let her sleep."

Maggie glanced up. "Look. I don't know what you're thinking, but we can't leave anybody with *them*. How would you like to be left behind if it was you?"

Jeanne's face changed. For a moment, she looked more like a savage animal than a girl. "I'd understand," she snarled. "Because that's the way it has to be. It's the law of the jungle, here. Only strong people survive. The weak ones . . ." She shook her head. "They're better off dead. And the faster you learn that, the more chance you'll have."

Maggie felt a spurt of horror and anger—and fear. Because Jeanne clearly knew the most about this place, and Jeanne might be right. They might all get caught because of one weak person who wouldn't make it anyway. . . .

She turned and looked at the lovely face again. Arcadia was Miles's age, eighteen or nineteen. And although she seemed to hear what Jeanne was saying—she'd turned her face that way—she didn't speak or argue. She didn't lose her still gentleness, either.

I can't leave her. What if Miles is alive but hurt somewhere, and somebody won't help him?

Maggie shot a glance at P.J. in her baseball cap. She was

young—she might be able to take care of herself, but that was all.

"Look, this isn't your problem," she finally said to Jeanne. "You just help P.J. get away safe, okay? You take care of her, and I'll be responsible for Cady."

"You'll be caught with Cady," Jeanne said flatly.

"Don't worry about it."

"I'm not. And I'm telling you right now; I'm not going to help you if you get in trouble."

"I don't *want* you to," Maggie said. She looked right into Jeanne's angry eyes. "Really. I don't want to wreck your chances, okay? But I'm not going to leave her."

Jeanne looked furious for another moment; then she shrugged. All the emotion drained from her face as if she were deliberately distancing herself. The bond she and Maggie had shared for that brief moment was severed.

She turned, looked through a crack behind her, then turned back.

"Fine," she said in a dull, indifferent tone. "Whatever you're going to do, you'd better get ready to do it now. Because the place is coming right up."

"Ready?" Maggie said.

They were all standing—or crouching, actually, since there wasn't room to straighten up—with their backs against the walls of the cart. Jeanne and P.J. on one side, Maggie on the other, with Cady in the corner.

"When I say go, you guys jump over here. Then all of us throw ourselves back that way," Maggie whispered.

Jeanne was peering out of the crack. "Okay, this is it," she said. "Now."

Maggie said, *"Go!"*

She had been a little worried that P.J. would freeze. But the moment the word was out of Maggie's mouth, Jeanne launched herself across the cart, crashing heavily into her, and P.J. followed. The cart rocked surprisingly hard and Maggie heard the groan of wood.

"Back!" she yelled, and everybody lunged the other way. Maggie hit a solid wall and knew she would have bruises, but the cart rocked again.

"Come on!" she yelled, and realized that they were all already coming on, throwing themselves to the other side in perfect sync. It was as if some flocking instinct had taken over and they were all three moving as one, throwing their weight alternately back and forth.

And the cart was responding, grinding to a halt and lurching off balance. It was like one of those party tricks where five or six people each use only two fingers to lift someone on a chair. Their combined force was impressive.

But not enough to tip the cart over. It was surprisingly well-balanced. And at any minute, Maggie realized, the people driving it were going to jump out and put a stop to it.

"Everybody—come on! Really hard! *Really hard!*" She was

yelling as if she were encouraging her soccer team. "We've got to do it, *now.*"

She launched herself at the other side as the cart began to sway that way, jumping as high as she could, hitting the wall as it reached the farthest point of its rock. She could feel the other girls flinging themselves with her; she could hear Jeanne giving a primal yell as she crashed into the wood.

And then there was a splintering sound, amazingly loud, amazingly long. A sort of groaning and shrieking that came from the wood itself, and an even louder scream of panic that Maggie realized must have come from the horses. The whole world was teetering and unstable—and suddenly Maggie was falling.

She hadn't known that it would be this violent, or this confusing. She wasn't sure of what was happening, except that there was no floor anymore and that she was engulfed in a deafening chaos of crashing and screeching and sobbing and darkness. She was being rolled over and over, with arms and legs that belonged to other people hitting her. A knee caught her in the nose, and for a few moments all she could think of was the pain.

And then, very suddenly, everything was still.

I think I killed us all, Maggie thought.

But then she realized she was looking at daylight—pale and feeble, but a big swathe of it. The cart was completely upside down and the doors at the back were hanging loose.

It did pop open, she thought. Just like those armored cars in the movies.

Outside, somebody was yelling. A man. Maggie had never heard such cold fury in a voice before. It cleared the last cobwebs out of her head.

"Come on! We've got to get out!"

Jeanne was already scrambling across the floor—which had previously been the ceiling—toward the hanging back doors.

"Are you okay? Come on, move, move!" Maggie yelled to P.J. "Follow her!"

A scared white face turned toward her, and then the younger girl was obeying.

Cady was lying in a heap. Maggie didn't wait for conversation, but grabbed her under the arms and hauled her into the light.

Once outside, she caught a glimpse of P.J. running and Jeanne beckoning. Then she tried to make sense of the scene around her. She saw a line of trees, their tops hidden in cloud-like vapors, their edges blurred by mist.

Mist, she thought. I remember . . .

But the thought was cut short almost before it was started. She found herself running, pounding toward the forest, nearly carrying Arcadia in her panic. The flat area she was running through was a sub-alpine meadow, the kind she'd often seen on hikes. In spring it would be a glorious mass of blue lupines and pink Indian paintbrush. Now it was just a tangle of old grass that slowed her down and tried to trip her.

"There they go! Get them!" the rough shout came behind her.

Don't look, she told herself. Don't slow down.

But she was looking, twisting her head over her shoulder. For the first time she saw what had happened to the cart.

It had fallen right off a narrow road and onto the sloping hillside below. They'd been lucky; only an outcrop of dark rock had stopped it from falling farther. Maggie was amazed to see how much damage there was—the cart looked like a splintered matchbox. Above, the horses seemed tangled in reins and shafts and fastenings; one of them was down and struggling frantically. Maggie felt a distant surge of remorse—she hoped its legs weren't broken.

There were also two men scrambling down the hillside.

They were the ones shouting. And one was pointing straight at Maggie.

Run, Maggie thought. Stop looking now. *Run.*

She ran into the forest, dragging Cady with her. They had to find a place to hide—underbrush or something. Maybe they could climb a tree. . . .

But one look at Cady and she realized how stupid *that* idea was. The smooth skin of the girl's face was clammy and luminous with sweat, her eyes were half shut, and her chest was heaving.

At least Jeanne and P.J. got away, Maggie thought.

Just then there was a crashing behind her, and a voice cursing. Maggie threw another glance back and found herself staring at a man's figure in the mist.

A scary man. The mist swirling behind him made him look eerie, supernatural, but it was more than that. He was *huge*, with shoulders as broad as a two-by-four, a massive chest, and heavily muscled arms. His waist was surprisingly narrow. His face was cruel.

"Gavin! I've got two of them!" he shouted.

Maggie didn't wait to hear more. She took off like a black-tailed deer.

And for a long time after that it was just a nightmare of running and being chased, stopping sometimes when she couldn't hold Cady up anymore, looking for places to hide. At one point, she and Cady were pressed together inside a hollow tree, trying desperately to get their breath back without making a sound, when their pursuers passed right by them. Maggie heard the crunch and squish of footsteps on ferns and started praying. She could feel Cady's heart beating hard, shaking them both, and she realized that Cady's lips were moving soundlessly.

Maybe she's praying, too, Maggie thought, and applied her eye to a crack in the tree.

There were two people there, horribly close, just a few feet away. One was the man she'd seen before and he was doing something bizarre, something that sent chills up her spine. He was turning his face this way and that with his eyes shut, his head twisting on a surprisingly long and supple neck.

As if he's *smelling* us out, Maggie thought, horrified.

Eyes still shut, the man said, "Do you sense anything?"

"No. I can't feel them at all. And I can't see them, with these trees for cover." It was a younger man who spoke, a boy really. He must be Gavin, Maggie thought. Gavin had dark blond hair, a thin nose, and a sharp chin. His voice was impatient.

"I can't feel them either," the big man said flatly, refusing to be hurried. "And that's strange. They can't have gotten too far away. They must be blocking us."

"I don't care what they're doing," Gavin said. "We'd better get them back fast. It's not like they were ordinary slaves. If we don't deliver that maiden we're dead. *You're* dead, Bern."

Maiden? Maggie thought. I guess in a place where they have slaves it's not weird to talk about maidens. But which girl does he mean? Not me; I'm not important.

"We'll get her back," Bern was saying.

"We'd better," Gavin said viciously. "Or I'm going to tell *her* that it was your fault. We were supposed to make sure this didn't happen."

"It hasn't happened yet," Bern said. He turned on his heel and walked into the mist. Gavin stared after him for a moment, and then followed.

Maggie let out her breath. She realized that Cady's lips had stopped moving.

"Let's go," she whispered, and took off in the opposite direction to the one the men had gone.

Then there was a time of endless running and pausing and listening and hiding. The forest was a terrible place. Around them was eerie twilight, made even spookier by the mist that lay in hollows and crept over fallen trees. Maggie felt as if she were in some awful fairy tale. The only good thing was that the dampness softened their footsteps, making it hard to track them.

But it was so quiet. No ravens, no gray jays. No deer. Just the mist and the trees, going on forever.

And then it ended.

Maggie and Cady suddenly burst out into another meadow. Maggie gave a frantic glance around, looking for shelter. Nothing. The mist was thinner here, she could see that there were no trees ahead, only an outcrop of rocks.

Maybe we should double back. . . .

But the voices were shouting in the forest behind them.

Above the rocks was a barren ledge. It looked like the end of a path, winding the other way down the mountain.

If we could get there, we'd be safe, Maggie thought. We could be around the corner in a minute, and out of sight.

Dragging Cady, she headed for the rocks. They didn't belong here; they were huge granite boulders deposited by some ancient glacier. Maggie clambered up the side of one easily, then leaned down.

"Give me your hand," she said rapidly. "There's a path up above us, but we've got to climb a little."

Cady looked at her.

Or—not looked, Maggie supposed. But she turned her face toward Maggie, and once again Maggie had the odd feeling that those blind eyes could somehow see better than most people's.

"You should leave me," Cady said.

"Don't be stupid," Maggie said. "Hurry up, give me your hand."

Cady shook her head. "You go," she said quietly. She seemed completely rational—and absolutely exhausted. She hadn't lost the tranquility that had infused her from the beginning, but now it seemed mixed with a gentle resignation. Her fine-boned face was drawn with weariness. "I'll just slow you down. And if I stay here, you'll have more time to get away."

"I'm not going to leave you!" Maggie snapped. "Come on!"

Arcadia remained for just a second, her face turned up to Maggie's, then her clear and luminous brown eyes filled. Her expression was one of inexpressible tenderness. Then she shook her head slightly and grabbed Maggie's hand—very accurately.

Maggie didn't waste time. She climbed as fast as she could, pulling Cady, rapping out breathless instructions. But the delay had cost them. She could hear the men getting nearer.

And when she reached the far end of the pile of boulders she saw something that sent shock waves through her system.

She was looking up a barren cliff face. There was no connection from the rocks to the ledge above. And below her, the hillside dropped off steeply, a hundred feet down into a gorge.

She'd led Cady right into a trap.

There was nowhere else to go.

CHAPTER 7

Maggie could have made it to the path above—if she'd been by herself. It was an easy climb, third level at most. But she wasn't alone. And there was no way to guide Arcadia up a cliff like that.

No time to double back to the forest, either.

They're going to get us, Maggie realized.

"Get down," she whispered to Cady. There was a hollow at the base of the boulder pile. It would only hold one of them, but at least it was shelter.

Even as she shoved Cady down into it, she heard a shout from the edge of the forest.

Maggie pressed flat against the rock. It was slippery with moss and lichen and she felt as exposed as a lizard on a wall. All she could do was hang on and listen to the sounds of two men getting closer and closer.

And closer, until Maggie could hear harsh breathing on the other side of the boulders.

"It's a dead end—" Gavin's young voice began.

"No. They're here." And that, of course, was Bern.

And then there was the most horrible sound in the world. The grunts of somebody climbing up rock.

We're caught.

Maggie looked around desperately for a weapon.

To her own amazement, she found one, lying there as if it had been left especially for her. A dried branch wedged in between the rocks above her. Maggie reached for it, her heart beating fast. It was heavier than it looked—the climate must be too wet here for anything to really dry out.

And the rocks are wet, too. Wet and slippery. And there's one good thing about this place—they'll have to come at us one at a time. Maybe I can push them off, one by one.

"Stay put," she whispered to Cady, trying to make her breath last to the end of that short sentence. "I've got an idea."

Cady looked beyond exhaustion. Her beautiful face was strained, her arms and legs were shaken by a fine trembling, and she was breathing in silent shudders. Her hair had come loose in a dark curtain around her shoulders.

Maggie turned back, her heart beating in her throat and her fingertips, and watched the top of the boulders.

But when what she was watching for actually came, she felt a terrible jolt, as if it were completely unexpected. She couldn't believe that she was seeing the close-cropped top of a man's head, then the forehead, then the cruel face. Bern. He was climbing like a spider, pulling himself by his fingertips. His huge shoulders appeared, then his barrel chest.

And he was looking right at Maggie. His eyes met hers, and his lips curved in a smile.

Adrenaline washed over Maggie. She felt almost disengaged from her body, as if she might float away from it. But she didn't faint. She stayed motionless as the terror buzzed through her like electricity—and she tightened her grip on the stick.

Bern kept smiling, but his eyes were dark and expressionless. As she looked into them, Maggie had no sense of connecting to another mind like hers.

He's not human. He's . . . something else, a distant part of her mind said with absolute conviction.

And then one of his legs came up, bulging with muscle under the jeans, and then he was pulling himself to stand, looming over her, towering like a mountain.

Maggie braced herself, gripping the stick. "Stay away from us."

"You've caused me a lot of trouble already," Bern said. "Now I'm going to show you something."

There was a little noise behind her. She glanced back in alarm and saw that it was Cady, trying to get up.

"Don't," Maggie said sharply. Cady couldn't, anyway. After a moment of trying to pull herself out of the hollow, she slumped down again, eyes shut.

Maggie turned back to see Bern lunging at her.

She thrust the stick out. It was completely instinctive. She didn't go for his head or his midsection; she jabbed at a fist-sized pit near his feet, turning the stick into a barrier to trip him.

It almost worked.

Bern's foot caught underneath it and his lunge became uncontrolled. Maggie saw him start to unbalance. But he wasn't the huge muscle-bound ape he looked like. In an instant he was recovering, throwing his weight sideways, jamming a foot to arrest his fall.

Maggie tried to get the stick unwedged, to use it again, but Bern was *fast*. He wrenched it out of her hand, leaving splinters in her palm. Then he threw it overhand, like a lance. Maggie heard it hit the ledge behind her with explosive force.

She tried to dodge, but it was already too late. Bern's big hand flashed forward, and then he had her.

He was holding her by both arms, looming over her.

"You trying to mess with me?" he asked in disbelief. "With *me*? Take a look at this."

His eyes weren't cold and emotionless now. Anger was streaming from him like the strong, hot scent of an animal. And then . . .

He changed.

It was like nothing Maggie had ever seen. She was staring at his face, trying to look defiant, when the features seemed to ripple. The coarse dark hair on his head *moved*, waves of it spreading down his face like fungus growing across a log. Maggie's stomach lurched in horror and she was afraid she was going to be sick, but she couldn't stop looking.

His eyes got smaller, the brown irises flowing out to cover the white. His nose and mouth thrust forward and his chin collapsed. Two rounded ears uncurled like awful flowers on top of his head. And when Maggie was able to drag her eyes from his face, she saw that his body had re-formed into a shapeless, hulking lump. His broad shoulders were gone, his waist was gone, his long legs bulging with muscle were squat little appendages close to the ground.

He was still holding Maggie tightly, but not with hands. With coarse paws that had claws on the ends and that were unbelievably strong. He wasn't a person at all anymore, but something huge and vaguely person-shaped. He was a black bear, and his shiny little pig-eyes stared into hers with animal enjoyment. He had a musky feral smell that got into Maggie's throat and made her gag.

I just saw a shapeshifter shift shape, Maggie thought with an astonishment that seemed dim and faraway. She was sorry she'd doubted Jeanne.

And sorry she'd blown it for Cady—and Miles. Sylvia had

been right. She was just an ordinary girl, only maybe extraordinarily stupid.

Down on the lower boulders, Gavin was laughing maliciously, watching as if this were a football game.

The bear opened his mouth, showing ivory-white teeth, darker at the roots, and lots of saliva. Maggie saw a string of it glisten on the hair of his jowl. She felt the paws flex on her arms, scooping her closer, and then—

Lightning hit.

That was what it looked like. A flash that blinded her, as bright as the sun, but blue. It crackled in front of her eyes, seeming to fork again and again, splitting and rejoining the main body of its energy. It seemed alive.

It was electrocuting the bear.

The animal had gone completely rigid, his head thrown back, his mouth open farther than Maggie would have believed possible. The energy had struck him just below what would have been the neck on a man.

Dimly, Maggie was aware of Gavin making a thin sound of terror. His mouth was open as wide as Bern's, his eyes were fixed on the lightning.

But it *wasn't* lightning. It didn't strike and stop. It kept on crackling into Bern, its form changing every second. Little electrical flickers darted through his bristling fur, crackling down his chest and belly and up around his muzzle. Maggie almost thought she could see blue flames in the cavern of his mouth.

Gavin gave a keening, inhuman scream and scrambled backward off the rocks, running.

Maggie didn't watch to see where he went. Her mind was suddenly consumed with one thought.

She had to make Bern let go of her.

She had no idea what was happening to him, but she did know that he was being killed. And that when he was dead he was going to topple off the mountain and take her with him.

She could *smell* burning now, the stink of smoking flesh and fur, and she could actually see white wisps rising from his coat. He was being cooked from the inside out.

I have to do something *fast*.

She squirmed and kicked, trying to get out of the grip of the paws that seemed to clutch her reflexively. She pushed and shoved at him, trying to get him to loosen his hold just an inch. It didn't work. She felt as if she were being smothered by a bearskin rug, a horrible-smelling pelt that was catching on fire. Why the lightning wasn't killing her, too, she didn't know. All she knew was that she was being crushed by his size and his weight and that she was going to die.

And then she gave a violent heave and kicked as hard as she could at the animal's lower belly. She felt the shock of solid flesh as her shin connected. And, unbelievably, she felt him recoil, stumbling back, his huge forelegs releasing her.

Maggie fell to the rock, instinctively spread-eagling and grabbing for holds to keep from sliding down the mountain.

Above her, the bear stood and quivered for another second, with that impossibly bright blue energy piercing him like a lance. Then, just as quickly as it had come, the lightning was gone. The bear swayed for a moment, then fell like a marionette with cut strings.

He toppled backward off the cliff into thin air. Maggie caught a brief glimpse of him hitting rock and bouncing and falling again, and then she turned her face away.

Her closed lids were imprinted with a blazing confusion of yellow and black afterimages. Her breath was coming so fast that she felt dizzy. Her arms and legs were weak.

What the *hell* was that?

The lightning had saved her life. But it was still the scariest thing she'd ever seen.

Some kind of magic. Pure magic. If I were doing a movie and I needed a special effect for magic, that's what I'd use.

She slowly lifted her head.

It had come from the direction of the ledge. When she looked that way, she saw the boy.

He was standing easily, doing something with his left arm—tying a handkerchief around a spot of blood at the wrist, it looked like. His face was turned partially away from her.

He's not much older than me, Maggie thought, startled. Or—is he? There was something about him, an assurance in the way he stood, a grim competence in his movements. It made him seem like an adult.

And he was dressed like somebody at a Renaissance Faire. Maggie had been to one in Oregon two summers ago, where everyone wore costumes from the Middle Ages and ate whole roast turkey legs and played jousting games. This boy was wearing boots and a plain dark cape and he could have walked right in and started sword fighting.

On the streets of Seattle, Maggie would have taken one look at him and grinned herself silly. Here, she didn't have the slightest urge to smile.

The Dark Kingdom, she thought. Slaves and maidens and shapeshifters—and magic. He's probably a wizard. What have I gotten myself into?

Her heart was beating hard and her mouth was so dry that her tongue felt like sandpaper. But there was something stronger than fear inside her. Gratitude.

"Thank you," she said.

He didn't even look up. "For what?" He had a clipped, brusque voice.

"For saving us. I mean—you did that, didn't you?"

Now he did look up, to measure her with a cool, unsympathetic expression. "Did what?" he said in those same unfriendly tones.

But Maggie was staring at him, stricken with sudden recognition that danced at the edges of her mind and then moved tantalizingly away.

I had a dream—didn't I? And there was somebody like you

in it. He looked like you, but his expression was different. And he said . . . he said that something was important. . . ."

She couldn't remember! And the boy was still watching her, waiting impatiently.

"That . . . thing." Maggie wiggled her fingers, trying to convey waves of energy. "That thing that knocked him off the cliff. You did that."

"The blue fire. Of course I did. Who else has the Power? But I didn't do it for you." His voice was like a cold wind blowing at her.

Maggie blinked at him.

She had no idea what to say. Part of her wanted to question him, and another part suddenly wanted to slug him. A third part, maybe smarter than both the others, wanted to run the way Gavin had.

Curiosity won out. "Well, why did you do it, then?" she asked.

The boy glanced down at the ledge he was standing on. "He threw a stick at me. Wood. So I killed him." He shrugged. "Simple as that."

He didn't throw it *at* you, Maggie thought, but the boy was going on.

"I couldn't care less what he was doing to you. You're only a slave. He was only a shapeshifter with the brain of a bear. Neither of you matter."

"Well—it doesn't matter why you did it. It still saved both

of us—" She glanced at Arcadia for confirmation—and broke off sharply.

"Cady?" Maggie stared, then scrambled over the rocks toward the other girl.

Arcadia was still lying in the hollow, but her body was now limp. Her dark head sagged bonelessly on her slender neck. Her eyes were shut; the skin over her face was drawn tight.

"Cady! Can you hear me?"

For a horrible second she thought the older girl was dead. Then she saw the tiny rise and fall of her chest and heard the faint sound of breathing.

There was a roughness to the breathing that Maggie didn't like. And at this distance she could feel the heat that rose from Cady's skin.

She's got a high fever. All that running and climbing made her sicker. She needs help, fast

Maggie looked back up at the boy.

He had finished with the handkerchief and was now taking the top off some kind of leather bag.

Suddenly Maggie's eyes focused. Not a leather bag; a canteen. He was tilting it up to drink.

Water.

All at once she was aware of her thirst again. It had been shoved to the back of her mind, a constant pain that could be forgotten while she was trying to escape from the slave traders. But now it was like a raging fire inside her. It was the most important thing in the world.

And Arcadia needed it even more than she did.

"Please," she said. "Can we have some of that? Could you drop it to me? I can catch it."

He looked at her quickly, not startled but with cool annoyance. "And how am I supposed to get it back?"

"I'll bring it to you. I can climb up."

"You can't," he said flatly.

"Watch me."

She climbed up. It was as easy as she'd thought; plenty of good finger- and toeholds.

When she pulled herself up onto the ledge beside him, he shrugged, but there was reluctant respect in his eyes.

"You're quick," he said. "Here." He held out the leather bag.

But Maggie was simply staring. This close, the feeling of familiarity was overwhelming.

It was *you* in my dream, she thought. Not just somebody like you.

She recognized everything about him. That supple, smoothly muscled body, and the way he had of standing as if he were filled with tightly leashed tension. That dark hair with the tiny waves springing out where it got unruly. That taut, grim face, those high cheekbones, that willful mouth.

And especially the eyes. Those fearless, black-lashed yellow eyes that seemed to hold endless layers of clear brilliance. That were windows on the fiercely intelligent mind behind them.

The only difference was the expression. In the dream, he had been anxious and tender. Here, he seemed joyless and bitter . . . and cold. As if his entire being were coated with a very thin layer of ice.

But it was *you*, Maggie thought. Not just somebody like you, because I don't think there *is* anybody like you.

Still lost in her memories, she said, "I'm Maggie Neely. What's your name?"

He looked taken aback. The golden eyes widened, then narrowed. "How dare you ask?" he rapped out. He sounded quite natural saying "How dare you," although Maggie didn't think she'd ever heard anybody say it outside of a movie.

"I had a dream about you," Maggie said. "At least—it wasn't *me* having the dream; it was more as if it was sent to me." She was remembering details now. "You kept telling me that I had to do something. . . ."

"I don't give a damn about your dreams," the boy said shortly. "Now, do you want the water or not?"

Maggie remembered how thirsty she was. She reached out for the leather bag eagerly.

He held on to it, not releasing it to her. "There's only enough for one," he said, still brusque. "Drink it here."

Maggie blinked. The bag did feel disappointingly slack in her grip. She tugged at it a little and heard a faint slosh.

"Cady needs some, too. She's sick."

"She's more than sick. She's almost gone. There's no point in wasting any on her."

I can't believe I'm hearing this again, Maggie thought. He's just like Jeanne.

She tugged at the bag harder. "If I want to share with her, that's my business, right? Why should it matter to you?"

"Because it's stupid. There's only enough for one."

"Look—"

"You're not afraid of me, are you?" he said abruptly. The brilliant yellow eyes were fixed on her as if he could read her thoughts.

It was strange, but she *wasn't* afraid, not exactly. Or, she *was* afraid, but something inside her was making her go on in spite of her fear.

"Anyway, it's my water," he said. "And I say there's only enough for one. You were stupid to try and protect her before, when you could have gotten away. Now you have to forget about her."

Maggie had the oddest feeling that she was being tested. But there was no time to figure out for what, or why.

"Fine. It's your water," she said, making her voice just as clipped as his. "And there's only enough for one." She pulled at the bag harder, and this time he let go of it.

Maggie turned from him, looked down at the boulders where Cady was lying. She judged the distance carefully, noting the way one boulder formed a cradle.

Easy shot. It'll rebound and wedge in that crack, she thought. She extended her arm to drop the bag.

"Wait!" The voice was harsh and explosive—and even more harsh was the iron grip that clamped on her wrist.

"What do you think you're doing?" the boy said angrily, and Maggie found herself looking into fierce yellow eyes.

CHAPTER 8

What are you doing?" he repeated ferociously. His grip was hurting her.

"I'm throwing the water bag down there," Maggie said. But she was thinking, He's so strong. Stronger than anybody I've ever met. He could break my wrist without even trying.

"I know that! *Why?*"

"Because it's easier than carrying it down in my teeth," Maggie said. But that wasn't the real reason, of course. The truth was that she needed to get temptation out of the way. She was so thirsty that it was a kind of madness, and she was afraid of what she would do if she held on to this cool, sloshing water bag much longer.

He was staring at her with those startling eyes, as if he were trying to pry his way into her brain. And Maggie had the odd feeling that he'd succeeded, at least far enough that he knew the real reason she was doing this.

"You are an idiot," he said slowly, with cold wonder. "You should listen to your body; it's telling you what it needs. You can't ignore thirst. You can't deny it."

"Yes, you can," Maggie said flatly. Her wrist was going numb. If this went on, she was going to drop the bag involuntarily, and in the wrong place.

"You can't," he said, somehow making the words into an angry hiss. "I should know."

Then he showed her his teeth.

Maggie should have been prepared.

Jeanne had told her. Vampires and witches and shapeshifters, she'd said. And Sylvia was a witch, and Bern had been a shapeshifter.

This boy was a vampire.

The strange thing was that, unlike Bern, he didn't get uglier when he changed. His face seemed paler and finer, like something chiseled in ice. His golden eyes burned brighter, framed by lashes that looked even blacker in contrast. His pupils opened and seemed to hold a darkness that could swallow a person up.

But it was the mouth that had changed the most. It looked even more willful, disdainful, and sullen—and it was drawn up into a sneer to display the fangs.

Impressive fangs. Long, translucent white, tapering into delicate points. Shaped like a cat's canines, with a sheen on them like jewels. Not yellowing tusks like Bern's, but delicate instruments of death.

What amazed Maggie was that although he looked completely different from anything she'd seen before, completely abnormal, he also looked completely natural. This was another kind of creature, just like a human or a bear, with as much right to live as either of them.

Which didn't mean she wasn't scared. But she was frightened in a new way, a way ready for action.

She was ready to fight, if fighting became necessary. She'd already changed that much since entering this valley: fear now made her not panicked but hyper alert.

If I have to defend myself I need both hands. And it's better not to let him see I'm scared.

"Maybe you can't ignore your kind of thirst," she said, and was pleased that her voice didn't wobble. "But I'm fine. Except that you're hurting my wrist. Can you please let go?"

For just an instant, the brilliant yellow eyes flared even brighter, and she wondered if he was going to attack her. But then his eyelids lowered, black lashes veiling the brightness. He let go of her wrist.

Maggie's arm sagged, and the leather bag dropped from her suddenly nerveless fingers. It landed safely at her feet. She rubbed her hand.

And didn't look up a moment later, when he said with a kind of quiet hostility, "Aren't you afraid of me?"

"Yes." It was true. And it wasn't just because he was a vampire or because he had a power that could send blue death twenty feet away. It was because of *him*, of the way he was. He was scary enough in and of himself.

"But what good is it, being afraid?" Maggie said, still rubbing her hand. "If you're going to try to hurt me, I'll fight back. And so far, you haven't tried to hurt me. You've only helped me."

"I told you, I didn't do it for *you*. And you'll never survive if you keep on being insane like this."

"Insane like what?" Now she did look up, to see that his eyes were burning dark gold and his fangs were gone. His mouth simply looked scornful and aristocratic.

"Trusting people," he said, as if it should have been obvious. "Taking care of people. Don't you know that only the strong ones make it? Weak people are deadweight—and if you try to help them, they'll drag you down with them."

Maggie had an answer for that. "Cady isn't weak," she said flatly. "She's *sick*. She'll get better—if she gets the chance. And if we don't take care of each other, what's going to happen to all of us?"

He looked exasperated, and for a few minutes they stared at each other in mutual frustration.

Then Maggie bent and picked up the bag again. "I'd better give it to her now. I'll bring your canteen back."

"Wait." His voice was abrupt and cold, unfriendly. But this time he didn't grab her.

"What?"

"Follow me." He gave the order briefly and turned without pausing to see if she obeyed. It was clear that he *expected* people to obey him, without questions. "Bring the bag," he said, without looking over his shoulder.

Maggie hesitated an instant, glancing down at Cady. But the hollow was protected by the overhanging boulders; Cady would be all right there for a few minutes.

She followed the boy. The narrow path that wound around the mountain was rough and primitive, interrupted by bands of broken, razor-sharp slate. She had to pick her way carefully around them.

In front of her, the boy turned toward the rock suddenly and disappeared. When Maggie caught up, she saw the cave.

The entrance was small, hardly more than a crack, and even Maggie had to stoop and go in sideways. But inside it opened into a snug little enclosure that smelled of dampness and cool rock.

Almost no light filtered in from the outside world. Maggie blinked, trying to adjust to the near-darkness, when there was a sound like a match strike and a smell of sulphur. A tiny flame was born, and Maggie saw the boy lighting some kind of crude stone lamp that had been carved out of the cave wall itself. He glanced back at her and his eyes flashed gold.

But Maggie was gasping, looking around her. The light of the little flame threw a mass of shifting, confusing shadows everywhere, but it also picked out threads of sparkling quartz in the rock. The small cave had become a place of enchantment.

And at the boy's feet was something that glittered silver. In the hush of the still air, Maggie could hear the liquid, bell-like sound of water dripping.

"It's a pool," the boy said. "Spring fed. The water's cold, but it's good."

Water. Something like pure lust overcame Maggie. She took three steps forward, ignoring the boy completely, and then her legs collapsed. She cupped a hand in the pool, felt the coolness encompass it to the wrist, and brought it out as if she were holding liquid diamond in her palm.

She'd never tasted anything as good as that water. No Coke she'd drunk on the hottest day of summer could compare with it. It ran through her dry mouth and down her parched throat—and then it seemed to spread all through her, sparkling through her body, soothing and reviving her. A sort of crystal clearness entered her brain. She drank and drank in a state of pure bliss.

And then, when she was in the even more blissful state of being not thirsty anymore, she plunged the leather bag under the surface to fill it.

"What's that for?" But there was a certain resignation in the boy's voice.

"Cady. I have to get back to her." Maggie sat back on

her heels and looked at him. The light danced and flickered around him, glinting bronze off his dark hair, casting half his face in shadow.

"Thank you," she said quietly, but in a voice that shook slightly. "I think you probably saved my life again."

"You were really thirsty."

"Yeah." She stood up.

"But when you thought there wasn't enough water, you were going to give it to her." He couldn't seem to get over the concept.

"Yeah."

"Even if it meant you dying?"

"I didn't die," Maggie pointed out. "And I wasn't planning to. But—yeah, I guess, if there wasn't any other choice." She saw him staring at her in utter bewilderment. "I took *responsibility* for her," she said, trying to explain. "It's like when you take in a cat, or—or it's like being a queen or something. If you say you're going to be responsible for your subjects, you are. You owe them afterward."

Something glimmered in his golden eyes, just for a moment. It could have been a dagger point of anger or just a spark of astonishment. There was a silence.

"It's not *that* weird, people taking care of each other," Maggie said, looking at his shadowed face. "Doesn't anybody do it here?"

He gave a short laugh. "Hardly," he said dryly. "The nobles

know how to take care of themselves. And the slaves have to fight each other to survive." He added abruptly, "All of which you should know. But of course you're not from here. You're from Outside."

"I didn't know if you *knew* about Outside," Maggie said.

"There isn't supposed to be any contact. There wasn't for about five hundred years. But when my—when the old king died, they opened the pass again and started bringing in slaves from the outside world. New blood." He said it simply and matter-of-factly.

Mountain men, Maggie thought. For years there had been rumors about the Cascades, about men who lived in hidden places among the glaciers and preyed on climbers. Men or monsters. There were always hikers who claimed to have seen Bigfoot.

And maybe they had—or maybe they'd seen a shapeshifter like Bern.

"And you think that's okay," she said out loud. "Grabbing people from the outside world and dragging them in here to be slaves."

"Not people. Humans. Humans are vermin; they're not intelligent." He said it in that same dispassionate tone, looking right at her.

"Are you *crazy*?" Maggie's fists were clenched; her head was lowered. Stomping time. She glared up at him through narrowed lashes. "You're talking to a human right now. Am I intelligent or not?"

"You're a slave without any manners," he said curtly. "And the law says I could kill you for the way you're talking to me."

His voice was so cold, so arrogant . . . but Maggie was starting not to believe it.

That couldn't be all there was to him. Because he was the boy in her dream.

The gentle, compassionate boy who'd looked at her with a flame of love behind his yellow eyes, and who'd held her with such tender intensity, his heart beating against hers, his breath on her cheek. That boy had been real—and even if it didn't make any sense, Maggie was somehow certain of it. And no matter how cold and arrogant this one seemed, they had to be part of each other.

It didn't make her less afraid of this one, exactly. But it made her more determined to ignore her fear.

"In my dream," she said deliberately, advancing a step on him, "you cared about at least one human. You wanted to take care of me."

"You shouldn't even be *allowed* to dream about me," he said. His voice was as tense and grim as ever, but as Maggie got closer to him, looking directly up into his face, he did something that amazed her. He fell back a step.

"Why not? Because I'm a slave? I'm a *person*." She took another step forward, still looking at him challengingly. "And I don't believe that you're as bad as you say you are. I think I saw what you were really like in my dream."

"You're crazy," he said. He didn't back up any farther; there was nowhere left to go. But his whole body was taut. "Why should I want to take care of you?" he added in a cold and contemptuous voice. "What's so special about you?"

It was a good question, and for a moment Maggie was shaken. Tears sprang to her eyes.

"I don't know," she said honestly. "I'm nobody special. There *isn't* any reason for you to care about me. But it doesn't matter. You saved my life when Bern was going to kill me, and you gave me water when you knew I needed it. You can talk all you want, but those are the facts. Maybe you just care about everybody, underneath. Or—"

She never finished the last sentence.

As she had been speaking to him, she was doing something she always did, that was instinctive to her when she felt some strong emotion. She had done it with P.J. and with Jeanne and with Cady.

She reached out toward him. And although she was only dimly aware that he was pulling his hands back to avoid her, she adjusted automatically, catching his wrists. . . .

And that was when she lost her voice and what she was saying flew out of her head. Because something happened. Something that she couldn't explain, that was stranger than secret kingdoms or vampires or witchcraft.

It happened just as her fingers closed on his hands. It was the first time they had touched like that, bare skin to bare skin.

When he had grabbed her wrist before, her jacket sleeve had been in between them.

It started as an almost painful jolt, a pulsating thrill that zigged up her arm and then swept through her body. Maggie gasped, but somehow she couldn't let go of his hand. Like someone being electrocuted, she was frozen in place.

The blue fire, she thought wildly. He's doing the same thing to me that he did to Bern.

But the next instant she knew that he wasn't. This wasn't the savage energy that had killed Bern, and it wasn't anything the boy was doing to her. It was something being done to both of them, by some incredibly powerful source outside either of them.

And it was trying . . . to open a channel. That was the only way Maggie could describe it. It was blazing a path open in her mind and connecting it to his.

She felt as if she had turned around and unexpectedly found herself facing another person's soul. A soul that was hanging there, without protection, already in helpless communication with hers.

It was by far the most intense thing that had ever happened to her. Maggie gasped again, seeing stars, and then her legs melted and she fell forward.

He caught her, but he couldn't stand up either. Maggie knew that as well as she knew what was going on in her own body. He sank to his knees, holding her.

What are you doing to me?

It was a thought, but it wasn't Maggie's. It was his.

I don't know . . . I'm not doing it . . . I don't understand!
Maggie had no idea how to send her thoughts to another person. But she didn't need to, it was simply happening. A pure
line of communication had been opened between them. It was
a fierce and terrible thing, a bit like being fused together by a
bolt of lightning, but it was also so wonderful that Maggie's
entire skin was prickling and her mind was hushed with awe.

She felt as if she'd been lifted into some new and wonderful place that most people never even saw. The air around her
seemed to quiver with invisible wings.

This is how people are supposed to be, she thought. *Joined
like this. Open to each other. With nothing hidden and no stupid
walls between them.*

A thought came back at her, sharp and quick as a hammer
strike. *No!*

It was so cold, so full of rejection, that for a moment
Maggie was taken aback. But then she sensed what else was
behind it.

Anger . . . and fear. He was afraid of this, and of her. He
felt invaded. Exposed.

Well, I do, too, Maggie said mentally. It wasn't that she
wasn't afraid. It was that her fear was irrelevant. The force that
held them was so much more powerful than either of them, so
immeasurably ancient, that fear was natural but not important.

The same light shone through each of them, stripping away their shields, making them transparent to each other.

It's all right for you. Because you *don't have anything to be ashamed of!* The thought flashed by so quickly that Maggie wasn't even sure she had heard it.

What do you mean? she thought. *Wait . . . Delos.*

That was his name. Delos Redfern. She knew it now, as unquestionably as she knew the names of her own family. She realized, too, as a matter of minor importance, an afterthought, that he was a prince. A vampire prince who'd been born to rule this secret kingdom, as the Redfern family had ruled it for centuries.

The old king was your father, she said to him. *And he died three years ago, when you were fourteen. You've been ruling ever since.*

He was pulling away from her mentally, trying to break the contact between them. *It's none of your business,* he snarled.

Please wait, Maggie said. But as she chased after him mentally, trying to catch him, to help him, something shocking and new happened, like a second bolt of lightning.

CHAPTER 9

She was in his mind. It was all around her, like a strange and perilous world. A terribly frightening world, but one that was full of stark beauty.

Everything was angles, as if she'd fallen into the heart of a giant crystal. Everything glittered, cold and clear and sharp. There were flashes of color as light shimmered and reflected, but for the most part it was dazzling transparency in every direction. Like the fractured ice of a glacier.

Really dangerous, Maggie thought. The spikes of crystal around her had edges like swords. The place looked as if it had never known warmth or soft color.

And you live *here?* she thought to Delos.

Go away. Delos's answering thought came to her on a wave of cold wind. *Get out!*

No, Maggie said. *You can't scare me. I've climbed glaciers before.* It was then that she realized what this place reminded her of. A summit. The bare and icy top of a mountain where no plants—and certainly no people—could survive.

But didn't anything *good ever happen to you?* she wondered. *Didn't you ever have a friend . . . or a pet . . . or something?*

No friends, he said shortly. *No pets. Get out of here before I hurt you.*

Maggie didn't answer, because even as he said it things were changing around her. It was as if the glinting surfaces of the nearby crystals were suddenly reflecting scenes, perfect little pictures with people moving in them. As soon as Maggie looked at one, it swelled up and seemed to surround her.

They were his memories. She was seeing bits of his childhood.

She saw a child who had been treated as a weapon from the time he was born. It was all about some prophecy. She saw men and women gathered around a little boy, four years old, whose black-lashed golden eyes were wide and frightened.

"No question about it," the oldest man was saying. Delos's teacher, Maggie realized, the knowledge flowing to her because Delos knew it, and she was in Delos's mind.

"This child is one of the Wild Powers," the teacher said, and his voice was full of awe—and fear. His trembling hands smoothed out a brittle piece of scroll. As soon as Maggie saw it she knew that the scroll was terribly old and had been kept in the Dark Kingdom for centuries, preserved here even when it was lost to the outside world.

"Four Wild Powers," the old man said, "who will be needed at the millennium to save the world—or to destroy it. The prophecy tells where they will come from." And he read:

"One from the land of kings long forgotten;
One from the hearth which still holds the spark;
One from the Day World where two eyes are watching;
One from the twilight to be one with the dark."

The child Delos looked around the circle of grim faces, hearing the words but not understanding them.

"'The land of kings, long forgotten,'" a woman was saying. "That must be the Dark Kingdom."

"Besides, we've seen what he can do," a big man said roughly. "He's a Wild Power, all right. The blue fire is in his blood. He's learned to use it too early, though; he can't control it. See?"

He grabbed a small arm—the left one—and held it up. It was twisted somehow, the fingers clawed and stiff, immobile.

The little boy tried to pull his hand away, but he was too weak. The adults ignored him.

"The king wants us to find spells to hold the power in," the woman said. "Or he'll damage himself permanently."

"Not to mention damaging us," the rough man said, and laughed harshly.

The little boy sat stiff and motionless as they handled him

like a doll. His golden eyes were dry and his small jaw was clenched with the effort not to give in to tears.

That's awful, Maggie said indignantly, aiming her thought at the Delos of the present. *It's a terrible way to grow up. Wasn't there anybody who cared about you? Your father?*

Go away, he said. *I don't need your sympathy.*

And your arm, Maggie said, ignoring the cold emptiness of his thought. *Is that what happens to it when you use the blue fire?*

He didn't answer, not in a thought directed at her. But another memory flashed in the facets of a crystal, and Maggie found herself drawn into it.

She saw a five-year-old Delos with his arm wrapped in what looked like splints or a brace. As she looked at it, she knew it wasn't just a brace. It was made of spells and wards to confine the blue fire.

"This is it," the woman who had spoken before was saying to the circle of men. "We can control him completely."

"Are you sure? You witches are careless sometimes. You're sure he can't use it at all now?" The man who said it was tall, with a chilly, austere face—and yellow eyes like Delos's.

Your father, Maggie said wonderingly to Delos. *And his name was . . . Tormentil? But . . .* She couldn't go on, but she was thinking that he didn't look much like a loving father. He seemed just like the others.

"Until I remove the wards, he can't use it at all. I'm sure, majesty." The woman said the last word in an everyday tone, but Maggie felt a little shock. Hearing somebody get called majesty—it made him *more* of a king, somehow.

"The longer they're left on, the weaker he'll be," the woman continued. "And *he* can't take them off himself. But I can, at any time—"

"And then he'll still be useful as a weapon?"

"Yes. But blood has to run before he can use the blue fire."

The king said brusquely, "Show me."

The woman murmured a few words and stripped the brace off the boy's arm. She took a knife from her belt and with a quick, casual motion, like Maggie's grandmother gutting a salmon, opened a gash on his wrist.

Five-year-old Delos didn't flinch or make a sound. His golden eyes were fixed on his father's face as blood dripped onto the floor.

"I don't think this is a good idea," the old teacher said. "The blue fire isn't meant to be used like this, and it damages his arm every time he does it—"

"Now," the king interrupted, ignoring him and speaking to the child for the first time. "Show me how strong you are, son. Turn the blue fire on . . ." He glanced up deliberately at the teacher. "Let's say—him."

"Majesty!" The old man gasped, backing against the wall.

The golden eyes were wide and afraid.

"Do it!" the king said sharply, and when the little boy shook his head mutely, he closed his hand on one small shoulder. Maggie could see his fingers tighten painfully. "Do what I tell you. *Now!*"

Delos turned his wide golden eyes on the old man, who was now shrinking and babbling, his trembling hands held up as if to ward off a blow.

The king changed his grip, lifted the boy's arm.

"Now, brat! *Now!*"

Blue fire erupted. It poured in a continuous stream like the water from a high-power fire hose. It struck the old man and spread-eagled him against the wall, his eyes and mouth open with horror. And then there *was* no old man. There was only a shadowy silhouette made of ashes.

"Interesting," the king said, dropping the boy's arm. His anger had disappeared as quickly as it had come. "Actually, I thought there would be more power. I thought it might take out the wall."

"Give him time." The woman's voice was slightly thick, and she was swallowing over and over.

"Well, no matter what, he'll be useful." The king turned to look at the others in the room. "Remember—all of you. A time of darkness is coming. The end of the millennium means the end of the world. But whatever happens outside, this kingdom is going to survive."

Throughout all of this, the little boy sat and stared at the place where the old man had been. His eyes were wide, the pupils huge and fixed. His face was white, but without expression.

Maggie struggled to breathe.

That's—that's the most terrible thing I've ever seen. She could hardly get the words of her thought out. *They made you kill your teacher—he made you do it. Your father.* She didn't know what to say. She turned blindly, trying to find Delos himself in this strange landscape, trying to talk to him directly. She wanted to look at him, to hold him. To comfort him. *I'm so sorry. I'm so sorry you had to grow up like that.*

Don't be stupid, he said. *I grew up to be strong. That's what counts.*

You grew up without anyone loving you, Maggie said.

He sent a thought like ice. *Love is for weak people. It's a delusion. And it can be deadly.*

Maggie didn't know how to answer. She wanted to shake him. *All that stuff about the end of the millennium and the end of the world—what did that mean?*

Exactly what it sounded like, Delos said briefly. *The prophecies are coming true. The world of humans is about to end in blood and darkness. And then the Night People are going to rule again.*

And that's why they turned a five-year-old into a lethal weapon? Maggie wondered. The thought wasn't for Delos, but she could feel that he heard it.

I am what I was meant to be, he said. *And I don't want to be anything else.*

Are you sure? Maggie looked around. Although she couldn't have described what she was doing, she knew what it was. She was looking for something . . . something to prove to him . . .

A scene flashed in the crystal.

The boy Delos was eight. He stood in front of a pile of boulders, rocks the size of small cars. His father stood behind him.

"Now!"

As soon as the king spoke, the boy lifted his arm. Blue fire flashed. A boulder exploded, disintegrating into atoms.

"Again!"

Another rock shattered.

"More power! You're not trying. You're useless!"

The entire pile of boulders exploded. The blue fire kept streaming, taking out a stand of trees behind the boulders and crashing into the side of a mountain. It chewed through the rock, melting shale and granite like a flamethrower burning a wooden door.

The king smiled cruelly and slapped his son on the back.

"That's better."

No. That's horrible, Maggie told Delos. *That's* wrong. *This is what it should be like.*

And she sent to him images of her own family. Not that the Neelys were anything special. They were like anybody. They had fights, some of them pretty bad. But there were lots of good times, too, and that was what she showed him. She showed him her life . . . herself.

Laughing as her father frantically blew on a flaming marshmallow on some long-past camping trip. Smelling turpentine and watching magical colors unfold on canvas as her mother painted. Perching dangerously on the handlebars of a bike while Miles pedaled behind her, then shrieking all the way down a hill. Waking up to a rough warm tongue licking her face, opening one eye to see Jake the Great Dane panting happily. Blowing out candles at a birthday party. Ambushing Miles from her doorway with a heavy-duty water rifle . . .

Who is that? Delos asked. He had been thawing; Maggie could feel it. There were so many things in the memories that were strange to him: yellow sunshine, modern houses, bicycles, machinery—but she could feel interest and wonder stir in him at the people.

Until now, when she was showing him a sixteen-year-old Miles, a Miles who looked pretty much like the Miles of today.

That's Miles. He's my brother. He's eighteen and he just started college. Maggie paused, trying to feel what Delos was thinking. *He's the reason I'm here. He got involved with this girl called Sylvia—I think she's a witch. And then he disappeared. I went to see Sylvia, and the next thing I know I'm waking up in a slave-trader's cart. In a place I never knew existed.*

Delos said, *I see.*

Delos, do you know him? Have you seen him before? Maggie tried to keep the question calm. She would have thought she could see anything that Delos was thinking, that it would all be reflected in the crystals around her, that there was nothing he could hide. But now suddenly she wasn't sure.

It's best for you to leave that alone, Delos said.

I can't, Maggie snapped back. *He's my brother! If he's in trouble I have to find him—I have to help him. That's what I've been trying to explain to you. We help each other.*

Delos said, *Why?*

Because we do. Because that's what people are supposed to do. And even you know that, somewhere down deep. You were trying to help me in my dream—

She could feel him pull away. *Your dreams are just your fantasies.*

Maggie said flatly, *No. Not this one. I had it before I met you.*

She could remember more of it now. Here in his mind the details were coming to her, all the things that had been unclear before. And there was only one thing to do.

She showed it to Delos.

The mist, the figure appearing, calling her name. The wonder and joy in his face when he caught sight of her. The way his hands closed on her shoulders, so gently, and the look of inexpressible tenderness in his eyes.

And then—I remember! Maggie said. *You told me to look for a pass, underneath a rock that looked like a wave about to break. You told me to get away from here, to escape. And then . . .*

She remembered what had happened then, and faltered.

And then he had kissed her.

She could feel it again, his breath a soft warmth on her cheek, and then the touch of his lips, just as soft. There had been so much in that kiss, so much of himself revealed. It had been almost shy in its gentleness, but charged with a terrible passion, as if he had known it was the last kiss they would ever share.

It was . . . so sad, Maggie said, faltering again. Not from embarrassment, but because she was suddenly filled with an intensity of emotion that frightened her. *I don't know what it meant, but it was so sad. . . .*

Then, belatedly, she realized what was happening with Delos.

He was agitated. Violently agitated. The crystal world around Maggie was trembling with denial and fury—and fear.

That wasn't me. I'm not like that, he said in a voice that was like a sword made of ice.

It was, she said, not harshly but quietly. *I don't understand it, but it really was you. I don't understand any of this. But there's a connection between us. Look what's happening to us right now. Is this normal? Do you people always fall into each other's minds?*

Get out! The words were a shout that echoed around Maggie from every surface. She could feel his anger; it was huge, violent, like a primal storm. And she could feel the terror that was underneath it, and hear the word that he was thinking and didn't want to think, that he was trying to bury and run away from.

Soulmates. That was the word. Maggie could sense what it meant. Two people connected, bound to each other forever, soul to soul, in a way that even death couldn't break. Two souls that were destined for each other.

It's a lie, Delos said fiercely. *I don't believe in souls. I don't love anyone. And I don't have any feelings!*

And then the world broke apart.

That was what it felt like. Suddenly, all around Maggie, the crystals were shattering and fracturing. Pieces were falling with the musical sound of ice. Nothing was stable, everything was turning to chaos.

And then, so abruptly that she lost her breath, she was out of his mind.

She was sitting on the ground in a small cave lit only by a dancing, flickering flame. Shadows wavered on the walls and ceiling. She was in her own body, and Delos was holding her in his arms.

But even as she realized it, he pulled away and stood up. Even in the dimness she could see that his face was pale, his eyes fixed.

As she got to her feet, she could see something else, too. It was strange, but their minds were still connected, even though he'd thrown her out of his world.

And what she saw . . . was herself. Herself through his eyes.

She saw someone who wasn't at all the frail blond princess type, not a bit languid and perfect and artificial. She saw a sturdy, rosy-brown girl with a straight gaze. A girl with autumn-colored hair, warm and vivid and real, and sorrel-colored eyes. It was the eyes that caught her attention: there was a clarity and honesty in them, a depth and spaciousness that made mere prettiness seem cheap.

Maggie caught her breath. Do *I* look like that? she wondered dizzily. I can't. I'd have noticed in the mirror.

But it was how he saw her. In his eyes, she was the only vibrant, living thing in a cold world of black and white. And she could feel the connection between them tightening, drawing him toward her even as he tried to pull farther away.

"No." His voice was a bare whisper in the cave. "I'm not bound to you. I don't love you."

"Delos—"

"I don't love anyone. I don't have feelings."

Maggie shook her head wordlessly. She didn't have to speak, anyway. All the time he was telling her how much he didn't love her, he was moving closer to her, fighting it every inch.

"You mean nothing to me," he raged through clenched teeth. "Nothing!"

And then his face was inches away from hers, and she could see the flame burning in his golden eyes.

"Nothing," he whispered, and then his lips touched hers.

CHAPTER 10

But at the instant that would have made it a kiss, Delos pulled away. Maggie felt the brush of his warm lips and then cold air as he jerked back.

"No," he said. "No." She could see the clash of fear and anger in his eyes, and she could see it suddenly resolve itself as the pain grew unbearable. He shuddered once, and then all the turmoil vanished, as if it were being swept aside by a giant hand. It left only icy determination in its wake.

"That's not going to help," Maggie said. "I don't even understand why you *want* to be this way, but you can't just squash everything down—"

"Listen," he said in a clipped, taut voice. "You said that in your dream I told you to go away. Well, I'm telling you the same thing now. Go away and don't ever come back. I never want to see your face again."

"Oh, fine." Maggie was trembling herself with frustration.

She'd had it; she'd finally reached the limit of her patience with him. There was so much bitterness in his face, so much pain, but it was clear he wasn't going to let anyone help.

"I mean it. And you don't know how much of a concession it is. I'm letting you go. You're not just an escaped slave, you're an escaped slave who knows about the pass in the mountains. The penalty for that is death."

"So kill me," Maggie said. It was a stupid thing to say and she knew it. He was dangerous—and the master of that blue fire. He could do it at the turn of an eyelash. But she was feeling stupid and reckless. Her fists were clenched.

"I'm telling you to leave," he said. "And I'll tell you something else. You wanted to know what happened to your brother."

Maggie went still. There was something different about him suddenly. He looked like somebody about to strike a blow. His body was tense and his eyes were burning gold like twin flames.

"Well, here it is," he said. "Your brother is dead. I killed him."

It *was* a blow. Maggie felt as if she'd been hit. Shock spread through her body and left her tingling with adrenaline. At the same time she felt strangely weak, as if her legs didn't want to hold her up any longer.

But she didn't believe it. She couldn't believe it, not just like that.

She opened her mouth and dragged in a breath to speak—
and froze.

Somewhere outside the cave a voice was calling. Maggie
couldn't make out the words, but it was a girl's voice. And it
was close . . . and coming closer.

Delos's head whipped around to look at the entrance of the
cave. Then, before Maggie could say anything, he was moving.

He took one step to the wall and blew out the flame of the
little stone lamp. Instantly, the cave was plunged into darkness.
Maggie hadn't realized how little light came from the entrance
crack—almost none at all.

No, she thought. Less light is coming through than before.
It's getting *dark*.

Oh, God, she thought. Cady.

I just walked off and left her there. What's wrong with me?
I forgot all about her—I didn't even think. . . .

"Where are you going?" Delos whispered harshly.

Maggie paused in mid rush and looked at him wildly. Or
looked *toward* him, actually, because now she couldn't see anything but darkness against paler darkness.

"To Cady," she said, distracted and frantic, clutching the
water bag she'd grabbed. "I left her down there. Anything
could have happened by now."

"You can't go outside," he said. "That's the hunting party I
came with. If they catch you I won't be able to help—"

"I don't care!" Maggie's words tumbled over his. "A minute

ago you never wanted to see me again. Oh, God, I *left* her. How could I do that?"

"It hasn't been that long," he hissed impatiently. "An hour or so." Vaguely, Maggie realized that he must be right. It seemed like a hundred years since she had climbed up to his ledge, but actually everything had happened quickly after that.

"I still have to go," she said, a little more calmly. "She's sick. And maybe Gavin came back." A wave of fear surged through her at the thought.

"If they catch you, you'll wish you were dead," he said distinctly. Before Maggie could answer, he was going on, his voice as brusque as ever. "Stay here. Don't come out until everybody's gone."

She felt the movement of air and the brush of cloth as he passed in front of her. The light from the entrance crack was cut off briefly, and then she saw him silhouetted for an instant against gray sky.

Then she was alone.

Maggie stood tensely for a moment, listening. The sound of her own breathing was too loud. She crept quietly to the entrance and crouched.

And felt a jolt. She could hear footsteps crunching on the broken slate outside. *Right* outside. Then a shadow seemed to fall across the crack and she heard a voice.

"Delos! What are you doing up here?"

It was a light, pleasant voice, the voice of a girl only a little

older than Maggie. Not a woman yet. And it was both concerned and casual, addressing Delos with a familiarity that was
startling.

But that wasn't what gave her the *big* jolt. It was that she
recognized the voice. She knew it and she hated it.

It was Sylvia.

She's here, Maggie thought. And from the way she's talking she's been here before—enough to get to know Delos. Or
maybe she was born here, and she's just started coming Outside.

Whatever the truth, it somehow made Maggie certain that
Miles had been brought here, too. But then—what? What
had happened to him after that? Had he done something that
meant he had to disappear? Or had it been Sylvia's plan from
the beginning?

Could Delos have really . . . ?

I don't believe it, Maggie thought fiercely, but there was a
pit of sick fear in her stomach.

Outside, Sylvia was chatting on in a musical voice. "We
didn't even know you'd left the group—but then we saw the
blue fire. We thought you might be in trouble—"

"Me?" Delos laughed briefly.

"Well—we thought there might *be* trouble," Sylvia amended.
Her own laugh was like wind chimes.

"I'm fine. I used the fire for practice."

"Delos." Sylvia's voice was gently reproving now, in a way

that was almost flirtatious. "You know you shouldn't do that. You'll only do more damage to your arm—it's never going to get better if you keep using it."

"I know." Delos's brusque tone was a sharp contrast to Sylvia's teasing. "But that's my business."

"I only want what's best for you—"

"Let's go. I'm sure the rest of the party is waiting for us."

He doesn't like her, Maggie thought. All her whinnying and prancing doesn't fool him. But I wonder what she is to him?

What she really wanted at that moment was to dash out and confront Sylvia. Grab her and shake her until she coughed up some answers.

But she'd already tried that once—and it had gotten her thrown into slavery. She gritted her teeth and edged closer to the entrance crack. It was dangerous and she knew it, but she wanted to see Sylvia.

When she did, it was another shock. Sylvia always wore slinky tops and fashionable jeans, but the outfit she had on now was completely medieval. More, she looked comfortable in it, as if these strange clothes were natural to her—and flattering.

She was wearing a sea-green tunic that had long sleeves and fell to the ground. Over that was another tunic, a shade paler, this one sleeveless and tied with a belt embroidered in green and silver. Her hair was loose in a fine shimmering mass, and she had a falcon on her wrist.

A real falcon. With a little leather hood on its head and leather ties with bells on its feet. Maggie stared at it, fascinated despite herself.

That whole fragile act Sylvia puts on, she thought. But you have to be *strong* to hold up a big bird like that.

"Oh, we don't have to rush back just yet," Sylvia was saying, moving closer to Delos. "Now that I'm here, we could go a little farther. This looks like a nice path; we could explore it."

Cady, Maggie thought. If they go to the end of the path, they'll see her. *Sylvia* will see her.

She had just decided to jump out of the cave when Delos spoke.

"I'm tired," he said in his flat, cold way. "We're going back now."

"Oh, you're tired," Sylvia said, and her smile was almost sly. "You see. I told you not to use your powers so much."

"Yes," Delos said, even more shortly. "I remember."

Before he could say anything else, Sylvia went on. "I forgot to mention, a funny thing happened. A guy named Gavin dropped in on the hunting party a little while ago."

Gavin.

Maggie's stomach plummeted.

He got away. And he saw everything.

And he must have moved *fast*, she thought absently. To hook around and get to a hunting party on the other side of this ledge—in time for Sylvia to come find Delos.

"You probably don't know him," Sylvia was saying. "But I do. He's the slave trader I use to get girls from Outside. He's normally pretty good, but today he was all upset. He said a group of slaves got loose on the mountain, and somehow his partner Bern got killed."

You . . . *witch*, Maggie thought. She couldn't think of a swear word strong enough.

Sylvia knew. There was no doubt about it. If Gavin was her flunky, and if he'd told her that Bern was dead, he must have told her the rest. That Bern had been killed by Prince Delos himself, fried with blue fire, and that there were two slave girls in front of Delos at the time.

She knew all along, Maggie thought, and she was just trying to trap Delos. But why isn't she afraid of him? He's the prince, after all. His father's dead; he's in charge. So how come she *dares* to set up her little traps?

"We were all concerned," Sylvia was going on, tilting her silvery head to one side. "All the nobles, and especially your great-grandfather. Loose slaves can mean trouble."

"How sweet of you to worry," Delos said. From what Maggie could see of his face, it was expressionless and his voice was dry and level. "But you shouldn't have. I used the fire for practice—on the other slave trader. Also on two slaves. They interrupted me when I wanted quiet."

Maggie sat in helpless admiration.

He did it. He outsmarted her. Now there's nothing she can

say. And there's no way to prove that he didn't kill us. Gavin ran; he couldn't have seen anything after that.

He saved us. Delos saved Cady and me both—again.

"I see." Sylvia bowed her head, looking sweet and placating, if not quite convinced. "Well, of course you had every right to do that. So the slaves are dead."

"Yes. And since they were only slaves, why are we standing here talking about them? Is there something about them I don't know?"

"No, no. Of course not," Sylvia said quickly. "You're right; we've wasted enough time. Let's go back."

In her mind, Maggie heard Gavin's voice. *It's not like they were ordinary slaves. If we don't deliver that maiden we're dead.*

So she's lying again, Maggie thought. What a surprise. But who's the maiden? And why's she so important?

For that matter, she thought, who's this great-grandfather of Delos's? When Sylvia mentioned him it sounded almost like a threat. But if he's a great-grandfather, he's got to be ancient. How are Sylvia and some old geezer teamed up?

It was an interesting question, but there was no time to think about it now. Sylvia and Delos were turning away from the cave, Sylvia murmuring about having to take a look at Delos's arm when they got back. In another moment they'd passed out of Maggie's line of sight and she heard the crunching noise of feet on slate.

Maggie waited until the last footstep faded, then she held

her breath and waited for a count of thirty. It was all she could stand. She ducked through the entrance crack and stood in the open air.

It was fully dark now. She was very nearly blind. But she could sense the vast emptiness of the valley in front of her, and the solidity of the mountain at her back.

And she should have felt relieved to be outside and not caught—but instead she felt strangely stifled. It took her a moment to realize why.

There was no sound at all. No footsteps, no voices, and no animals, either. And that was what felt eerie. It might be too cold at night for mosquitoes and gnats and flies, but there should have been *some* animal life to be heard. Birds heading into the trees to rest, bats heading out. Deer feeding. Bucks charging around—it was autumn, after all.

There was nothing. Maggie had the unnerving feeling that she was alone in a strange lifeless world swathed in cotton, cut off from everything real.

Don't stick around and think about it, she told herself sternly. Find Cady. Now!

Gritting her teeth, she thrust the water bag into her jacket and started back. By keeping close to the mountain's bulk on her left and feeling ahead with her foot before each step, she could find her way in the dark.

When she reached the ledge, her stomach tightened in dismay.

Terrific. Going down in pitch darkness—there's going to be no way to see the footholds. Oh, well, I'll feel for them. The worst that can happen is I fall a hundred feet straight down.

"Cady," she whispered. She was afraid to talk too loudly; the hunting party might be anywhere and sound could carry surprisingly well on a mountain slope.

"Cady? Are you okay?"

Her heart thumped slowly five times before she heard something below. Not a voice, just a stirring, like cloth on rock, and then a sigh.

Relief flooded through Maggie in a wave that was almost painful. Cady hadn't died or been abducted because Maggie had left her. "Stay there," she whispered as loudly as she dared. "I'm coming down. I've brought water."

It wasn't as hard going down as she'd expected. Maybe because she was still high on adrenaline, running in survival mode. Her feet seemed to find the toeholds of their own accord and in a few minutes she was on the boulders.

"Cady." Her fingers found warmth and cloth. It moved and she heard another little sigh. "Cady, are you okay? I can't see you."

And then the darkness seemed to lighten, and Maggie realized that she *could* see the shape she was touching, dimly but distinctly. She glanced up and went still.

The moon was out. In a sky that was otherwise covered with clouds, there was a small opening, a clear spot. The moon shone down through it like a supernatural white face, nearly full.

"Maggie." The voice was a soft breath, almost a whisper, but it seemed to blow peace and calm into Maggie's heart. "Thanks for letting me rest. I feel stronger now."

Maggie looked down. Silver light touched the curves of Cady's cheek and lips. The blind girl looked like some ancient Egyptian princess, her dark hair loose in crimped waves around her shoulders, her wide, heavy-lashed eyes reflecting the moon. Her face was as serene as ever.

"I'm sorry it took so long. I got some water," Maggie said. She helped Cady sit up and put the water bag to her lips.

She doesn't look as feverish, Maggie thought as Cady was drinking. Maybe she can walk. But where? Where can we *go*?

They would never make it to the pass. And even if they did, what then? They'd be high on a mountain—some mountain— in the dark and cold of a November night.

"We need to get you to a doctor," she said.

Cady stopped drinking and gave the bag back. "I don't think there's anything like that here. There might be some healing woman down there in the castle—but . . ." She stopped and shook her head. "It's not worth it."

"What do you mean, it's not worth it? And, hey, you're really feeling better, aren't you?" Maggie added, pleased. It was the first time Cady had gotten out more than a few words. She sounded very weak, but rational, and surprisingly knowledgeable.

"It's not worth it because it's too much of a risk. *I'm* too much of a risk. You have to leave me here, Maggie. Go down and get to shelter yourself."

"Not this again!" Maggie waved a hand. She really couldn't deal with this argument anymore. "If I left you up here, you'd die. It's going to get freezing cold. So I'm not going to leave you. And if there's a healing woman down at the castle, then we're going to the castle. Wherever the castle is."

"It's the place all the Night People are," Arcadia said, unexpectedly grim. "The slaves, too. Everybody who lives here is inside the castle gates; it's really like a little town. And it's exactly the place you shouldn't go."

Maggie blinked. "How come you know so much? Are you an escaped slave like Jeanne?"

"No. I heard about it a year or so ago from someone who had been here. I was coming here for a reason—it was just bad luck that I got caught by the slave traders on my way in."

Maggie wanted to ask her more about it, but a nagging voice inside her said that this wasn't the time. It was already getting very cold. They couldn't be caught on the mountainside overnight.

"That road the cart was on—does it go all the way to the castle? Do you know?"

Cady hesitated. She turned her face toward the valley, and Maggie had the strange sense that she was looking out.

"I think so," she said at last. "It would make sense that it does, anyway—there's only one place to go in the valley."

"Then we've got to find it again." Maggie knew that wouldn't be easy. They'd run a long way from Bern and Gavin. But she knew the general direction. "Look, even if we don't get to the castle, we should find the road so we know where we are. And if we have to spend the night on the mountain, it's much better to be in the forest. It'll be warmer."

"That's true. But—"

Maggie didn't give her a chance to go on. "Can you stand up? I'll help—put your arm around my neck. . . ."

It was tricky, getting Cady out of the nest of boulders. She and Maggie both had to crawl most of the way. And although Cady never complained, Maggie could see how tired it made her.

"Come on," Maggie said. "You're doing great." And she thought, with narrowed eyes and set teeth, If it comes to that, I'll *carry* her.

Too many people had told her to leave this girl. Maggie had never felt quite this stubborn before.

But it wasn't easy. Once into the woods, the canopy of branches cut off the moonlight. In only minutes, Cady was leaning heavily on Maggie, stumbling and trembling. Maggie herself was stumbling, tripping over roots, slipping on club moss and liverwort.

Strangely, Cady seemed to have a better sense of direction than she did, and in the beginning she kept murmuring, "This way, I think." But after a while she stopped talking, and some time after that, she stopped even responding to Maggie's questions.

At last, she stopped dead and swayed on her feet.

"Cady—"

It was no good. The taller girl shivered once, then went limp. It was all Maggie could do to break her fall.

And then she was sitting alone in a small clearing, with the spicy aroma of red cedar around her, and an unconscious girl in her lap. Maggie held still and listened to the silence.

Which was broken suddenly by the crunch of footsteps.

Footsteps coming toward her.

It might be a deer. But there was something hesitant and stealthy about it. Crunch, pause; crunch, pause. The back of Maggie's neck prickled.

She held her breath and reached out, feeling for a rock or a stick—*some* weapon. Cady was heavy in her lap.

Something stirred in the salal bushes between two trees. Maggie strained her eyes, every muscle tense.

"Who's there?"

CHAPTER 11

The bushes stirred again. Maggie's searching fingers found only acorns and licorice fern, so she made a fist instead, sliding out from underneath Cady and holding herself ready.

A form emerged from the underbrush. Maggie stared so hard she saw gray dots but she couldn't tell anything about it.

There was a long, tense moment, and then a voice came to her.

"I told you you'd never make it."

Maggie almost fainted with relief.

At the same moment the moon came out from behind a cloud. It shone down into the clearing and over the slender figure standing with a hand on one hip. The pale silvery light turned red hair almost black, but the angular face and narrowed skeptical eyes were unmistakable. Not to mention the sour expression.

Maggie let out a long, shuddering breath. "Jeanne!"

"You didn't get very far, did you? The road's just over there. What happened? Did she drop dead on you?"

It was amazing how good that irritable, acerbic voice sounded to Maggie. She laughed shakily. "No, Cady's not dead. *Bern's* dead—you know, the big slave trader guy. But—"

"You're joking." Jeanne's voice sharpened with respect and she moved forward. "You killed him?"

"No. It was—look, I'll explain later. First, can you help me get her to somewhere more protected? It's really getting freezing out here, and she's completely out."

Jeanne leaned down, looking at Arcadia. "I told you before I wasn't going to help you if you got in trouble."

"I know," Maggie said. "Can you sort of pick her up from that side? If we both get an arm under her shoulders she might be able to walk a little."

"Bull," Jeanne said shortly. "We'd better chair-carry her. Link hands and we can get her up."

Maggie clasped a cold, slender hand with calluses and a surprisingly firm grip. She heaved weight, and then they were carrying the unconscious girl.

"You're strong," she grunted.

"Yeah, well, that's one of the side benefits of being a slave. The road's this way."

It was awkward, slow work, but Maggie was strong, too, and Jeanne seemed to be able to guide them around the worst of the underbrush. And it was so good just to be with another human being who was healthy and clearheaded and didn't want to kill her, that Maggie felt almost lighthearted.

"What about P.J.? Is she okay?"

"She's fine. She's in a place I know—it's not much, but it's shelter. That's where we're going."

"You took care of her," Maggie said. She shook her head in the darkness and laughed.

"What are you snickering about?" Jeanne paused and they spent a few minutes maneuvering around a fallen log covered with spongy moss.

"Nothing," Maggie said. "It's just—you're pretty nice, aren't you? Underneath."

"I look out for myself first. That's the rule around here. And don't you forget it," Jeanne said in a threatening mutter. Then she cursed as her foot sank into a swampy bit of ground.

"Okay," Maggie said. But she could still feel a wry and wondering smile tugging up the corner of her mouth.

Neither of them had much breath for talking after that. Maggie was in a sort of daze of tiredness that wasn't completely unpleasant. Her mind wandered.

Delos . . . she had never met anyone so confusing. Her entire body reacted just at the thought of him, with frustration and anger and a longing that she didn't understand. It was a physical pang.

But then *everything* was so confusing. Things had happened so fast since last night that she'd never had time to get her mental balance. Delos and the incredible thing that had happened between them was only one part of the whole mess.

He said he'd killed Miles. . . .

But that couldn't be true. Miles couldn't be dead. And Delos wasn't capable of anything like that. . . .

Was he?

She found that she didn't want to think about that. It was like a huge dark cloud that she didn't want to enter.

Wherever Jeanne was taking her, it was a long, cold trek. And a painful one. After about fifteen minutes Maggie's arms began to feel as if they were being pulled out of the sockets, and a hot spot of pain flared at the back of her neck. Her sweat was clammy running down her back and her feet were numb.

But she wouldn't give up, and Jeanne didn't either. Somehow they kept going. They had traveled for maybe about forty-five minutes, with breaks, when Jeanne said, "Here it is."

A clearing opened in front of them, and moonlight shone on a crude little shack made of weathered wood. It leaned dangerously to one side and several boards were missing, but it had a ceiling and walls. It was shelter. To Maggie, it looked beautiful.

"Runaway slaves built it," Jeanne said breathlessly as they took the last few steps to the cabin. "The Night People hunted them down, of course, but they didn't find this place. All the slaves at the castle know about it." Then she called in a slightly louder tone, "It's me! Open the door!"

A long pause, and then there was the sound of a wooden bolt sliding and the door opened. Maggie could see the pale blob of a small face. P.J. Penobscot, with her red plaid baseball cap still on backward and her slight body tense, was blinking sleepy, frightened eyes.

Then she focused and her face changed.

"Maggie! You're okay!" She flung herself at Maggie like a small javelin.

"Ow—hey!" Maggie swayed and Cady's limp body dipped perilously.

"I'm glad to see you, too," Maggie said. To her own surprise, she found herself blinking back tears. "But I've got to put this girl down or I'm going to drop her."

"Back here," Jeanne said. The back of the cabin was piled with straw. She and Maggie eased Arcadia down onto it and then P.J. hugged Maggie again.

"You got us out. We got away," P.J. said, her sharp little chin digging into Maggie's shoulder.

Maggie squeezed her. "Well—we all got us out, and Jeanne helped get you away. But I'm glad everybody made it."

"Is she . . . all right?" P.J. pulled back and looked down at Arcadia.

"I don't know." Cady's forehead felt hot under Maggie's

hand, and her breathing was regular but with a rough, wheezy undertone Maggie didn't like.

"Here's a cover," Jeanne said, dragging up a piece of heavy, incredibly coarse material. It seemed as big as a sail and so rigid it hardly sagged or folded. "If we all get under it, we can keep warm."

They put Cady in the middle, Maggie and P.J. on one side of her and Jeanne on the other. The cover was more than big enough to spread over them.

And the hay smelled nice. It was prickly, but Maggie's long sleeves and jeans protected her. There was a strange comfort in P.J.'s slight body cuddled up next to her—like a kitten, Maggie thought. And it was so blessedly good to *not* be moving, to not be carrying anyone, but just to sit still and relax her sore muscles.

"There was a little food stashed here," Jeanne said, digging under the hay and pulling out a small packet. "Dried meat strips and oatcakes with salal berries. We'd better save some for tomorrow, though."

Maggie tore into the dried meat hungrily. It didn't taste like beef jerky; it was tougher and gamier, but right at the moment it seemed delicious. She tried to get Cady to eat some, but it was no use. Cady just turned her head away.

She and Jeanne and P.J. finished the meal off with a drink of water, and then they lay back on the bed of hay.

Maggie felt almost happy. The gnawing in her stomach

was gone, her muscles were loosening up, and she could feel a warm heaviness settling over her.

"You were going . . . to tell me about Bern . . . ," Jeanne said from the other side of Cady. The words trailed off into a giant yawn.

"Yeah." Maggie's brain was fuzzy and her eyes wouldn't stay open. "Tomorrow . . ."

And then, lying on a pile of hay in a tiny shack in a strange kingdom, with three girls who had been strangers to her before this afternoon and who now seemed a little like sisters, she was fast asleep.

Maggie woke up with her nose cold and her feet too hot. Pale light was coming in all the cracks in the boards of the cabin. For one instant she stared at the rough weathered-silver boards and the hay on the floor and wondered where she was. Then she remembered everything.

"Cady." She sat up and looked at the girl beside her.

Cady didn't look well. Her face had the waxy inner glow of somebody with a fever, and there were little tendrils of dark hair curled damply on her forehead. But at Maggie's voice her eyelashes fluttered, then her eyes opened.

"Maggie?"

"How are you feeling? Want some water?" She helped Cady drink from the leather bag.

"I'm all right. Thanks to you, I think. You brought me

here, didn't you?" Cady's face turned as if she were looking around the room with her wide, unfocused eyes. She spoke in short sentences, as if she were conserving her strength, but her voice was more gentle than weak. "And Jeanne, too. Thank you both."

She must have heard us talking last night, Maggie thought. Jeanne was sitting up, straw in her red hair, her green eyes narrow and alert instantly. P.J. was stirring and making grumpy noises.

"Morning," Maggie said. "Is everybody okay?"

"Yeah," P.J. said in a small, husky voice. There was a loud rumble from her stomach. "I guess I'm still a little hungry," she admitted.

"There're a couple oatcakes left," Jeanne said. "And one strip of meat. We might as well finish it off."

They made Cady eat the meat, although she tried to refuse it. Then they divided the oatcakes solemnly into four parts and ate them, chewing doggedly on dry, flaky mouthfuls.

"We're going to need more water, too," Maggie said, after they'd each had a drink. The leather bag was almost empty. "But I think the first thing is to figure out what we're going to do now. What our plan is."

"The first thing," Jeanne said, "is to tell us what happened to Bern."

"Oh." Maggie blinked, but she could see why Jeanne would want to know. "Well, he's definitely dead." She sketched in what had happened after she and Cady had started running through the woods. How Gavin and Bern had chased them and had finally driven them into a corner on the boulder pile. How Bern had climbed up and changed . . .

"He was a shapeshifter, you know," she said.

Jeanne nodded, unsurprised. "Bern means bear. They usually have names that mean what they are. But you're saying you tried to fight *that* guy off with a stick? You're dumber than I thought." Still, her green eyes were gleaming with something like wry admiration, and P.J. was listening with awe.

"And then—there was this lightning," Maggie said. "And it killed Bern, and Gavin ran away." She realized, even as she said it, that she didn't want to tell everything that had happened with Delos. She didn't think Jeanne would understand. So she left out the way their minds had linked when they touched, and the way she'd seen his memories—and the fact that she'd dreamed about him before ever coming to this valley.

"Then I filled the water bag and we heard Sylvia coming and he went out to make sure she didn't find me or Cady," she finished. She realized that they were all staring at her. Cady's face was thoughtful and serene as always, P.J. was scared but interested in the story—but Jeanne was riveted with disbelief and horror.

"You're saying *Prince Delos* saved your life? With the blue fire? You're saying he didn't turn you over to the hunting party?" She said it as if she were talking about Dracula.

"It's the truth." Good thing I didn't tell her about the kiss, Maggie thought.

"It's impossible. Delos hates everybody. He's the most dangerous of all of them."

"Yeah, that's what he kept telling me." Maggie shook her head. The way Jeanne was looking at her made her uncomfortable, as if she were defending someone unredeemably evil. "He also said at one point that he killed my brother," she said slowly. "But I didn't know whether to believe it. . . ."

"Believe it." Jeanne's nostrils were flared and her lip curled as if she were looking at something disgusting. "He's the head of this whole place and everything that goes on here. There's nothing he wouldn't do. I can't believe he let you go." She considered for a moment, then said grimly, "Unless he's got something special in mind. Letting you go and then hunting you down later. It's the kind of thing he'd enjoy."

Maggie had a strange feeling of void in her stomach that had nothing to do with hunger. She tried to speak calmly. "I don't think so. I think—he just didn't care if I got away."

"You're fooling yourself. You don't understand about these people because you haven't been here. *None* of you have been here." Jeanne looked at P.J., who was watching with wide blue eyes, and at Cady, who was listening silently, her head slightly bowed. "The Night People are *monsters*. And the ones here in the Dark Kingdom are the worst of all. Some of them have been alive for hundreds of years—some of them were here when Delos's grandfather founded the place. They've been holed up in this valley all that time . . . and *all they do is hunt.* It's their only sport. It's all they care about. It's all they *do.*"

Maggie's skin was prickling. Part of her didn't want to pursue this subject any further. But she had to know.

"Last night I noticed something weird," she said. "I was standing outside and listening, but I couldn't hear any animal sounds anywhere. None at all."

"They've wiped them out. All the animals in the wild are gone."

P.J.'s thin little hand clutched at Maggie's arm nervously. "But then what do they hunt?"

"Animals they breed and release. I've been a slave here for three years, and at first I only saw them breeding local animals—cougars and black bears and wolverines and stuff. But in the last couple of years they've started bringing in exotics. Leopards and tigers and things."

Maggie let out her breath and patted P.J.'s hand. "But not humans."

"Don't make me laugh. Of course humans—but only when they can get an excuse. The laws say the vampires can't hunt slaves to death because they're too precious—pretty soon the food supply would be gone. But if slaves get loose, they at least get to hunt them down and bring them back to the castle. And if a slave has to be executed, they do a death hunt."

"I see." The void in Maggie's stomach had become a yawning chasm. "But—"

"If he let you go, it was so he could come back and hunt you," Jeanne said flatly. "I'm telling you, he's *bad.* It was three years ago that the old king died and Delos took over, okay? And it was three years ago that they started bringing new slaves in. Not just grabbing people off the mountain if they got too close, but actually going down and kidnapping girls off the streets. That's why I'm *here.* That's why P.J.'s here."

Beside Maggie, P.J. shivered. Maggie put an arm around her and felt the slight body shaking against hers. She gulped, her other hand clenching into a fist. "Hey, kiddo. You've been really brave so far, so just hang on, okay? Things are going to work out."

She could feel Jeanne's sarcastic eyes on her from beyond Cady, daring her to explain exactly *how* things were going to work out. She ignored them.

"Was it the same for you, Cady?" she asked. She was glad to get off the subject of Delos, and she was remembering the strange thing Cady had said last night. *I was coming here for a reason. . . .*

"No. They got me on the mountain." But the way Cady spoke alarmed Maggie. It was slowly and with obvious effort, the voice of someone who had to use all their strength just to concentrate.

Maggie forgot all about Delos and the slave trade and put a

hand to Cady's forehead. "Oh, God," she said. "You're burning up. You're totally on fire."

Cady blinked slowly. "Yes—it's the poison," she said in a foggy voice. "They injected me with something when they caught me—but I had a bad reaction to it. My system can't take it."

Adrenaline flicked through Maggie. "And you're getting worse." When Cady nodded reluctantly, she said, "Right. Then there's no choice. We have to get to the castle because that's where the healing women are, right? If anybody can help, they can, right?"

"Wait a minute," Jeanne said. "We can't go down to the castle. We'd be walking right into their arms. And we can't get out of the valley. I found the pass before, but that was by acci-dent. I couldn't find it again—"

"I could," Maggie said. When Jeanne stared at her, she said, "Never mind how. I just can. But going that way means climbing down a mountain on the other side and Cady can't make it. And I don't think she'll make it if we leave her alone here and go look for help."

Jeanne's narrow green eyes were on her again, and Maggie knew what they were saying. *So we've got to give up on her. It's the only thing that makes sense.* But Maggie bulldozed on in determination. "*You* can take P.J. to the pass—I can tell you how to get there—and I'll take Cady to the castle. How about that? If you can tell me how to get to *it*."

"It stinks," Jeanne said flatly. "Even if you make it to the castle with her hanging on you, you won't know how to get in. And if you *do* get in, you'll be committing suicide—"

She broke off, and everyone started. For an instant Maggie didn't understand why—all she knew was that she had a sudden feeling of alarm and alertness. Then she realized that Cady had turned suddenly toward the door. It was the quick, instinctive gesture of a cat who has heard something dangerous, and it triggered fear in the girls who were learning to live by their own instincts.

And now that Maggie sat frozen, she could hear it, too, faraway but distinct. The sound of people calling, yelling back and forth. And another sound, one that she'd only heard in movies, but that she recognized instantly. Hounds baying.

"It's them," Jeanne whispered into the dead silence of the shack. "I told you. They're hunting us."

"With *dogs*?" Maggie said, shock tingling through her body.

"It's all over," Jeanne said. "We're dead."

CHAPTER 12

No, we're not!" Maggie said. She kicked the heavy cover off and jumped up, grabbing Cady's arm. "Come on!"

"Where?" Jeanne said.

"The castle," Maggie said. "But we've got to stick together." She grabbed P.J.'s arm with her other hand.

"The castle?"

Maggie pinned Jeanne with a look. "It's the only thing that makes sense. They'll be expecting us to try to find the pass, right? They'll find us if we stay here. The only place they *won't* expect us to go is the castle."

"You," Jeanne said, "are completely crazy—"

"Come on!"

"But you just might be right." Jeanne grabbed Cady from the other side as Maggie started for the door.

"You stay right behind us," Maggie hissed at P.J.

The landscape in front of her looked different than it had last night. The mist formed a silver net over the trees, and although there was no sun, the clouds had a cool pearly glow.

It was beautiful. Still alien, still disquieting, but beautiful.

And in the valley below was a castle.

Maggie stopped involuntarily as she caught sight of it. It rose out of the mist like an island, black and shiny and solid. With towers at the edges. And a wall around it with a saw-toothed top, just like the castles in pictures.

It looks so real, Maggie thought stupidly.

"Don't stand there! What are you waiting for?" Jeanne snapped, dragging at Cady.

Maggie tore her eyes away and made her legs work. They headed at a good pace straight for the thickest trees below the shack.

"If it's dogs, we should try to find a stream or something, right?" she said to Jeanne. "To cut off our scent."

"I know a stream," Jeanne said, speaking in short bursts as they made their way through dew-wet ferns and saxifrages. "I lived out here a while the first time I escaped. When I was looking for the pass. But they're not just dogs."

Maggie helped Cady scramble over the tentacle-like roots of a hemlock tree. "What's that supposed to mean?"

"It means they're shapeshifters, like Bern and Gavin. So they don't just track us by scent. They also feel our life energy."

Maggie thought about Bern turning his face this way and that, saying, *"Do you sense anything?"* And Gavin saying, *"No. I can't feel them at all."*

"Great," Maggie muttered. She glanced back and saw P.J. following doggedly, her face taut with concentration.

It was a strange sort of chase. Maggie and her group were trying to keep as quiet as possible, which was made easier by the dampness of the rain forest around them. Although there were four of them moving at once, the only sound from close up was the soft pant of quick breathing and the occasional short gasp of direction from Jeanne.

They slipped and plunged and stumbled between the huge dark trunks that stood like columns in the mist. Cedar boughs drooped from above, making it twilight where Maggie was trying to pick her way around moss-covered logs. There was a cool green smell like incense everywhere.

But however still the world was around them, there was always the sound of the hounds baying in the distance. Always behind them, always getting closer.

They crossed an icy, knee-deep stream, but Maggie didn't have much hope that it would throw the pursuit off. Cady began to lag seriously after that. She seemed dazed and only semiconscious, following instructions as if she were sleepwalking, and only answering questions with a fuzzy murmur. Maggie was worried about P.J., too. They were all weak with hunger and shaky with stress.

But it wasn't until they were almost at the castle that the hunt caught up with them.

They had somehow finished the long, demanding trek down the mountain. Maggie was burning with pride for P.J. and Cady. And then, all at once, the baying of the hounds came, terribly close and getting louder fast.

At the same moment, Jeanne stopped and cursed, staring ahead.

"What?" Maggie was panting heavily. "You see them?"

Jeanne pointed. "I see the *road*. I'm an idiot. They're coming right down it, much faster than we can go through the underbrush. I didn't realize we were headed for it."

P.J. leaned against Maggie, her slight chest heaving, her plaid baseball hat askew.

"What are we going to do?" she said. "Are they going to catch us?"

"No!" Maggie set her jaw grimly. "We'll have to go back fast—"

At that moment, faintly but distinctly, Cady said, "The tree."

Her eyes were half shut, her head was bowed, and she still looked as if she were in a trance. But for some reason Maggie felt she ought to listen to her.

"Hey, wait—look at this." They were standing at the foot of a huge Douglas fir. Its lowest branches were much too high to climb in the regular way, but a maple had fallen against it and remained wedged, branches interlocked with the giant, forming a steep but climbable ramp. "We can go up."

"You're *crazy*," Jeanne said again. "We can't possibly hide here; they're going to go right by us. And besides, how does she even *know* there's a tree here?"

Maggie looked at Arcadia. It was a good question, but Cady wasn't answering. She seemed to be in a trance again.

"I don't know. But we can't just stand around and wait for them to come." The truth was that her instincts were all standing up and screaming at her, and they said to trust. "Let's try it, okay? Come on, P.J., can you climb that tree?"

Four minutes later they were all up. We're hiding in a Christmas tree, Maggie thought as she looked out between sprays of flat aromatic needles. From this height she could see the road, which was just two wheel tracks with grass growing down the middle.

Just then the hunt arrived.

The dogs came first, dogs as big as Jake the Great Dane, but leaner. Maggie could see their ribs clearly defined under their short, dusty tan coats. Right behind them were people on horses.

Sylvia was at the front of the group.

She was wearing what looked like a gown split for riding, in a cool shade of glacier green. Trotting beside her stirrup was Gavin, the blond slave trader who'd chased Maggie and Cady yesterday and had run to tattle when Delos killed Bern with the blue fire.

Yeah, they're buddy-buddy all right, Maggie thought. But she didn't have time to dwell on it. Coming up fast behind Sylvia were two other people who each gave her a jolt, and she didn't know which shock was worse.

One was Delos. He was riding a beautiful horse, so dark brown it was almost black, but with reddish highlights. He sat straight and easy in the saddle, looking every inch the elegant young prince. The only discordant note was the heavy brace on his left arm.

Maggie stared at him, her heart numb.

He *was* after them. It was just as Jeanne had said. He was hunting them down with dogs. And he'd probably told Sylvia that he hadn't really killed two of the slaves.

Almost inaudibly, Jeanne breathed, "You see?"

Maggie couldn't look at her.

Then she saw another rider below and froze in bewilderment.

It was Delos's father.

He looked exactly the way he had in Delos's memories. A tall man, with blood-red hair and a cold, handsome face. Maggie couldn't see his eyes at this distance, but she knew that they were a fierce and brilliant yellow.

The old king. But he was *dead.* Maggie was too agitated to be cautious.

"Who is that? The red-haired man," she murmured urgently to Jeanne.

Jeanne answered almost without a sound. "Hunter Redfern."

"It's not the king?"

Jeanne shook her head minutely. Then, when Maggie kept staring at her, she breathed. "He's Delos's great-grandfather. He just came. I'll tell you about it later."

Maggie nodded. And the next instant it was swept out of her head as P.J.'s hand clutched at her and she felt a wave of adrenaline.

The party below was stopping.

The hounds turned and circled first, forming a hesitant clump not twenty feet down the road. When the people pulled up their horses they were almost directly below Maggie's tree.

"What is it?" the tall man said, the one Jeanne had called Hunter Redfern.

And then one of the hounds changed. Maggie caught the movement out of the corner of her eye and looked quickly, or she would have missed it.

The lean, wiry animal reared up, like a dog trying to look over a fence. But when it reached its full height it didn't wobble or go back down. It steadied, and its entire dusty-tan body rippled.

Then, as if it were the most natural thing in the world, its shoulders went back and its arms thickened. Its spine straightened and it seemed to gain more height. Its tail pulled in and disappeared. And its hound face melted and re-formed, the ears and muzzle shrinking, the chin growing.

In maybe twenty seconds the dog had become a boy, a boy who still wore patches of tan fur here and there, but definitely human-looking.

And he's got pants on, Maggie thought distractedly, even though her heart was pounding in her throat. I wonder how they manage that?

The boy turned his head toward the riders. Maggie could see the ribs in his bare chest move with his breathing.

"Something's wrong here," he said. "I can't follow their life force anymore."

Hunter Redfern looked around. "Are they blocking it?"

Gavin spoke up from beside Sylvia's stirrup. "Bern said they were blocking it yesterday."

"Isn't that impossible?" Delos's cool voice came from the very back of the group, where he was expertly holding his nervous, dancing horse in check. "If they're only humans?"

Hunter didn't move or blink an eye, but Maggie saw a glance pass between Sylvia and Gavin. She herself twisted her head slightly, just enough to look at the other girls in the tree.

She wanted to see if Jeanne understood what they were talking about, but it was Cady who caught her eye. Cady's eyes were shut, her head leaning against the dark furrowed trunk of the tree. Her lips were moving, although Maggie couldn't hear any sound.

And Jeanne was watching her with narrowed eyes and an expression of grim suspicion.

"Human vermin are full of surprises," Hunter Redfern was saying easily down below. "It doesn't matter. We'll get them eventually."

"They may be heading for the castle," Sylvia said. "We'd better put extra guards at the gate."

Maggie noticed how Delos stiffened at that.

And so did Hunter Redfern, even though he was looking the other way. He said calmly, "What do you think of that, Prince Delos?"

Delos didn't move for an instant. Then he said, "Yes. Do it." But he said it to a lean, bearded man beside him, who bowed his head in a quick jerk.

And he did something that made Maggie's heart go cold.

He looked up at her.

The other people in his party, including the hounds, were looking up and down the road, or sideways into the forest at their own level. Delos was the only one who'd been sitting quietly, looking straight ahead. But now he tilted his chin and turned an expressionless face toward the cluster of branches where Maggie was sitting.

And met her gaze directly.

She saw the blaze of his yellow eyes, even at this distance. He was looking coolly and steadily—at her.

Maggie jerked back and barely caught herself from falling. Her heart was pounding so hard it was choking her. But she didn't seem to be able to do anything but cling to her branch.

We're dead, she thought dizzily, pinned into immobility by those golden eyes. He's stronger than the rest of them; he's a Wild Power. And he could sense us all along.

Now all they have to do is surround the tree. We can try to fight—but we don't have weapons. They'll beat us in no time. . . .

Go away. The voice gave her a new shock. It was clear and unemotional—and it was in Maggie's head.

Delos? she thought, staring into that burning gaze. *You can—?*

His expression didn't change. *I told you before, but you wouldn't listen. What do I have to do to make you understand?*

Maggie's heart picked up more speed. *Delos, listen to me. I don't want—*

I'm warning you, he said, and his mental voice was like ice. *Don't come to the castle. If you do, I won't protect you again.*

Maggie felt cold to her bones, too numb to even form words to answer him.

I mean it, he said. *Stay away from the castle if you want to stay alive.*

Then he turned away and Maggie felt the contact between them broken off cleanly. Where his presence had been, she could feel emptiness.

"Let's go," he said in a short, hard voice, and spurred his horse forward.

And then they were all moving, heading on down the path,

leaving Maggie trying to keep her trembling from shaking the tree.

When the last horse was out of sight, P.J. let out her breath, sagging. "I thought they had us," she whispered.

Maggie swallowed. "Me, too. But Cady was right. They went on by." She turned. "Just what was that stuff about us blocking them?"

Cady was still leaning her head against the tree trunk, and her eyes were still closed. But she seemed almost asleep now— and her lips weren't moving.

Jeanne's eyes followed Maggie's. They were still narrowed, and her mouth was still tight with something like grim humor. But she didn't say anything. After a moment she quirked an eyebrow and shrugged minutely. "Who knows?"

You know, Maggie thought. At least more than you're telling me. But there was something else bothering her, so she said, "Okay, then, what about that guy who looks like Delos's father? Hunter Redfern."

"He's a bigwig in the Night World," Jeanne said. "Maybe the biggest. It was his son who founded this place back in the fourteen hundreds."

Maggie blinked. "In the *whats?*"

Jeanne's eyes glowed briefly, sardonically. "In the fourteen hundreds," she said with exaggerated patience. "They're vampires, all right? Actually, they're lamia, which is the kind of vampire that can have kids, but that's not the point. The point is they're immortal, except for accidents."

"That guy has been alive more than five hundred years," Maggie said slowly, looking down the path where Hunter Redfern had disappeared.

"Yeah. And, yeah, everybody says how much he looks like the old king. Or the other way around, you know."

Delos sure thinks he looks like him, Maggie thought. She'd seen the way Hunter handled Delos, guiding him as expertly as Delos had guided his horse. Delos was *used* to obeying somebody who looked and sounded just like Hunter Redfern.

Then she frowned. "But—how come *he* isn't king?"

"Oh . . ." Jeanne sighed and ducked under a spray of fir needles that was tangled in her hair. She looked impatient and uneasy. "He's from the Outside, okay? He's only been here a couple of weeks. All the slaves say that he didn't even know about this place before that."

"He didn't know . . ."

"Look. This is the way I heard it from the old slaves, okay? Hunter Redfern had a son named Chervil when he was really young. And when Chervil was, like, our age, they had some big argument and got estranged. And then Chervil ran off with his friends, and that left Hunter Redfern without an heir. And Hunter Redfern never knew that where the kid went was *here*." Jeanne gestured around the valley. "To start his own little kingdom of Night People. But then somehow Hunter found out, so he came to visit. And that's why he's here."

She finished and stretched her shoulders, looking down the tree-ramp speculatively. P.J. sat quietly, glancing from Jeanne to Maggie. Cady just breathed.

Maggie chewed her lip, not satisfied yet. "He's here just to visit? That's all?"

"I'm a slave. You think I asked him personally?"

"I think you *know*."

Jeanne stared at her a moment, then glanced at P.J. Her look was almost sullen, but Maggie understood.

"Jeanne, she's been through hell already. Whatever it is, she can take it. Right, kiddo?"

P.J. twisted her plaid cap in a complete circle and settled it more firmly on her head. "Right," she said flatly.

"So tell us," Maggie said. "What's Hunter Redfern doing here?"

CHAPTER 13

I think," Jeanne said, "that he's here to get Delos to close the Dark Kingdom out. Shut up the castle and come join him Outside. And, incidentally, of course, kill all the slaves."

Maggie stared. "Kill them all?"

"Well, it makes sense. Nobody would need them anymore."

"And that's why you were escaping now," Maggie said slowly.

Jeanne gave her a quick, startled glance. "You're really not as stupid as you seem at first sight, you know?"

"Gee, thanks." Maggie shifted on her branch. A minute ago she'd been thinking how good it would feel to get away from the twigs poking her. Now she suddenly wanted to stay here forever, hiding. She had a *very* bad feeling.

"So why," she said, forming her thoughts slowly, "does Hunter Redfern want to do this right now?"

"What do *you* think? Really, Maggie, what do you know about all this?"

Four Wild Powers, Maggie thought, hearing Delos's old teacher's voice in her mind. *Who will be needed at the millennium, to save the world—or to destroy it.*

"I know that something's happening at the millennium, and that Delos is a Wild Power, and that the Wild Powers are supposed to do something—"

"Save the world," Jeanne said in a clipped voice. "Except that that's not what the Night People want. They figure there's going to be some huge catastrophe that'll wipe out most of the humans—and then *they* can take over. And that's why Hunter Redfern's here. He wants the Wild Powers on his side instead of on the humans'. He wants them to help destroy the human world instead of saving it. And it looks like he's just about convinced Delos."

Maggie let out a shaky breath and leaned her head against a branch. It was just like what Delos had told her—except that Jeanne was an uninterested party. She still wanted not to believe it, but she had a terrible sinking feeling. In fact, she had a strange feeling of *weight,* as if something awful were trying to settle on her shoulders.

"The millennium really means the end of the world," she said.

"Yeah. Our world, anyway."

Maggie glanced at P.J., who was swinging her thin legs over the edge of a branch. "You still okay?"

P.J. nodded. She looked frightened, but not unbearably so. She kept her eyes on Maggie's face trustingly.

"And do *you* still want to go to the castle?" Jeanne said, watching Maggie just as closely. "Hunter Redfern is a very bad guy to mess with. And I hate to tell you, but your friend Prince Delos is out for our blood just like the rest of them."

"No, I don't still *want* to go," Maggie said briefly. Her head went down and she gave Jeanne a brooding look under her eyelashes. "But I have to, anyway. I've got even more reasons now."

"Such as?"

Maggie held up a finger. "One, I've got to get help for Cady." She glanced at the motionless figure clinging trancelike to the fir's trunk, then held up another finger. "Two, I have to find out what happened to my brother." Another finger. "And, three, I have to get those slaves free before Hunter Redfern has them all killed."

"You have to *what?*" Jeanne said in a muffled shriek. She almost fell out of the tree.

"I kind of thought you'd react that way. Don't worry about it. You don't have to get involved."

"I was wrong before. You *are* as dumb as you look. And you are totally freaking crazy."

Yeah, I know, Maggie thought grimly. It's probably just as well I didn't mention the fourth reason.

Which was that she had to keep Delos from aiding and

abetting the end of the world. That was the responsibility that had settled on her, and she had no idea why it was hers except that she'd been inside his mind. She *knew* him. She couldn't just walk away.

If anybody could talk to him about it and convince him not to do it, she could. She had absolutely no doubt about that. So it was her job to try.

And if he was really as evil as Jeanne seemed to think—if it was true that he'd killed Miles . . . well, then she had a different job.

She had to do whatever was necessary to stop him. Distant and impossible as it seemed, she would have to kill him if that was what it took.

"Come on," she said to the other girls. "Cady, do you think you can climb down now? And, Jeanne, do you know a way into the castle?"

The moat stank.

Maggie had been glad to find Jeanne knew a way into the castle. That was before she discovered that it involved swimming through stagnant water and climbing up what Jeanne called a garderobe but what was all too obviously the shaft of an old latrine.

"Just kill me, somebody," Maggie whispered halfway up. She was soaking wet and daubed with unthinkable slime. She couldn't remember ever being quite this dirty.

The next moment she forgot about it in her worry about Cady. Cady had managed the swim, still doing everything she was told as if she were in a trance. But now she was getting shaky. Maggie wondered seriously whether this sort of activity was helpful to somebody who'd been poisoned.

When they were finally at the top of the shaft, Maggie looked around and saw a small room that seemed to be built directly into the castle wall. Everything was made of dark stone, with a cold and echoing feel to it.

"Don't make any noise," Jeanne whispered. She bent close to Maggie, who was helping support Cady. "We need to go down a passage and through the kitchen, okay? It's all right if slaves see us, but we have to watch out for *them*."

"We've got to get Cady to a healing woman—"

"I know! That's where I'm trying to take you." Jeanne clamped a hand on P.J.'s shoulder and steered her into a corridor.

More stone. More echoes. Maggie tried to walk without her shoes squishing or smacking. She was dimly impressed with the castle itself—it was grand and cold and so huge that she felt like an insect making her way through the passage.

After what seemed like an endless walk, they emerged in a small entryway partitioned off by wooden screens. Maggie could hear activity behind the screens, and as Jeanne led them stealthily forward, she caught a glimpse of people moving on the other side. They were spreading white tablecloths over long wooden tables in a room that seemed bigger than Maggie's entire house.

Another doorway. Another passage. And finally the kitchen, which was full of bustling people. They were stirring huge iron cauldrons and turning meat on spits. The smell of a dozen different kinds of food hit Maggie and made her feel faint. She was so hungry that her knees wobbled and she had to swallow hard.

But even more than hungry, she was scared. They were in plain sight of dozens of people.

"Slaves," Jeanne said shortly. "They won't tell on us. Grab a sack to wrap around you and come on. And, P.J., take off that ridiculous hat."

Slaves, Maggie thought, staring. They were all dressed identically, in loose-fitting pants and tops that were like short tunics. Jeanne was wearing the same thing—it had looked enough like clothes from Outside that Maggie hadn't really focused on it before. What struck her now was that everybody looked so . . . un-ironed. There were no sharp creases. And no real color. All the clothes were an indeterminate shade of beige-brown, and all the faces seemed just as dull and faded. They were like drones.

What would it be like to live that way? she wondered as she threw a rough sack around her shoulders to hide the dark blue of her jacket. Without any choice in what you do, and any hope for the future?

It would be terrible, she decided. And it might just drive you crazy.

I wonder if any of them ever . . . snap?

But she couldn't look around anymore. Jeanne was hustling through a doorway into the open air. There was a kind of garden here just outside the kitchen, with scraggly fruit trees and what looked like herbs. Then there was a courtyard and finally a row of huts nestled against the high black wall that surrounded the castle.

"This is the really dangerous part," Jeanne whispered harshly. "It's the back, but if one of *them* looks out and sees us, we're in trouble. Keep your head down—and walk like this. Like a slave." She led them at a shuffling run toward a hut.

This place *is* like a city, Maggie thought. A city inside a wall, with the castle in the middle.

They reached the shack. Jeanne pulled the door open and bustled them inside. Then she shut the door again and sagged.

"I think we actually made it." She sounded surprised.

Maggie was looking around. The tiny room was dim, but she could see crude furniture and piles of what looked like laundry. "This is it? We're safe?"

"Nowhere is safe," Jeanne said sharply. "But we can get some slave clothes for you here, and we can rest. And I'll go get the healing woman," she added as Maggie opened her mouth.

While she was gone, Maggie turned to Cady and P.J. They

were both shivering. She made Cady lie down and had P.J. help her go through one of the piles of laundry.

"Get your wet things off," Maggie said. She pulled off her own hightops and shrugged out of her sodden jacket. Then she knelt to get Cady's shoes off. The blind girl was lying motionless on a thin pallet, and didn't respond to Maggie's touch. Maggie was worried about her.

Behind her, the door opened and Jeanne came in with two people. One was a gaunt and handsome woman, with dark hair pulled untidily back and an apron over her tunic and pants. The other was a young girl who looked frightened.

"This is Laundress." The way Jeanne said it, it was clearly a proper name. "She's a healer, and the girl's her helper."

Relief washed through Maggie. "This is Cady," she said. And then, since nobody moved and Cady couldn't speak for herself, she went on, "She's from Outside, and she was poisoned by the slave traders. I'm not sure how long ago that was—at least a couple of days. She's been running a high fever and most of the time she's just sort of sleepwalking—"

"What is this?" The gaunt woman took a step toward Cady, but her expression was anything but welcoming. Then she turned on Jeanne angrily, "How could you bring this— thing—in here?"

Maggie froze where she was by Cady's feet. "What are you talking about? She's sick—"

"She's one of them!" The woman's eyes were burning

darkly at Jeanne. "And don't tell me you didn't notice. It's perfectly plain!"

"*What's* perfectly plain?" Maggie's fists were clenched. "Jeanne, what's she talking about?"

The woman's burning eyes turned on her. "This girl is a witch."

Maggie went still.

Part of her was amazed and disbelieving. A witch? Like Sylvia? A Night Person?

Cady wasn't at all like that. She wasn't evil. She was *normal*, a nice, ordinary, gentle girl. She *couldn't* be anything supernatural. . . .

But another part of Maggie wasn't even startled. It was saying that at some deep level she had known all along.

Her mind was bringing up pictures. Cady in the hollow tree, when she and Maggie were hiding from Bern and Gavin. Cady's lips moving—and Gavin saying *I can't feel them at all.*

The hound today had said the same thing. *I can't follow their life force anymore.*

She was blocking them from sensing us, Maggie thought. And she was the one who told us to climb the tree. She's blind, but she can see things.

It's true.

She turned slowly to look at the girl lying on the pallet.

Cady was almost perfectly still, her breathing barely lifting her chest. Her hair was coiled around her head like damp snakes, her face was smudged and dirty, her lashes spiky on her cheeks. But somehow she hadn't lost any of her serene beauty. It remained untouched, whatever happened to her body.

I don't care, Maggie thought. She may be a witch, but she's not like Sylvia. I *know* she's not evil.

She turned back to Laundress, and spoke carefully and deliberately.

"Look, I understand that you don't like witches. But this girl has been with us for two days, and all she's done is help us. And, I mean, look at her!" Maggie lost her reasonable tone. "They were bringing her here as a slave! She wasn't getting any special treatment. She's not on their side!"

"Too bad for her," Laundress said. Her voice was flat and . . . plain. The voice of a woman who saw things in black and white and didn't like arguments.

And who knew how to back up her beliefs. One big gaunt hand went beneath her apron, into a hidden pocket. When it came out again, it was gripping a kitchen knife.

"Wait a minute," Jeanne said.

Laundress didn't look at her. "Friends of witches are no friends of ours," she said in her plain, heavy way. "And that includes you."

With one motion, Jeanne wheeled away from her and into a fighting stance. "You're right. I knew what she was. I hated her, too, at first. But it's like Maggie told you. She's not going to hurt us!"

"I'm not going to miss a chance to kill one of *them*," Laundress said. "And if you try to stop me, you'll be sorry."

Maggie's heart was pounding. She looked back and forth from the tall woman, who was holding the knife menacingly, to Jeanne, who was crouched with her teeth bared and her eyes narrowed. They were ready to fight.

Maggie found herself in the middle of the room, in a triangle formed by Cady and Jeanne and the knife. She was too angry to be frightened.

"You *put that down*," she said to Laundress fiercely, forgetting that she was speaking to an adult. "You're not going to do anything with that. How can you even try?"

Vaguely, she noticed movement behind the woman. The frightened young girl who hadn't said anything so far was stepping forward. She was staring at Maggie, pointing at Maggie. Her eyes and mouth were wide open, but her voice was an indrawn breath.

"The Deliverer!"

Maggie hardly heard the gasped words. She was rushing on. "If you people don't stick together, what kind of chance do you have? How can you ever get free—"

"It's her!" This time the girl shrieked it, and nobody could help but hear. She clutched at Laundress's arm wildly. "You heard what she said, Laundress. She's come to free us."

"What are you talking a—?" Jeanne broke off, looking at Maggie with her eyebrows drawn together. Suddenly the eyebrows flew up and she straightened slightly from her crouch, "Hmm."

Maggie stared back. Then she followed all their eyes and looked down at herself in bewilderment.

For the first time since she'd arrived in the Dark Kingdom she wasn't wearing her jacket and her shoes. She was wearing exactly what she'd been wearing when her mother's screams woke her three days before—her flowered pajama top, wrinkled jeans, and mismatched socks.

"'She will come clothed in flowers, shod in blue and scarlet,'" the girl was saying. She was still pointing at Maggie, but now it was with something like reverence. "And she will speak of freedom.' You heard her, Laundress! It's *her*. She's the one!"

The knife trembled slightly. Maggie stared at the red knuckles of the hand holding it, then looked up at Laundress's face.

The blotchy features were grim and skeptical—but there was an odd gleam of half-stifled hope in the eyes. "Is she the one?" she said harshly to Jeanne. "Is this idiot Soaker right? Did she say she's come to deliver us?"

Jeanne opened her mouth, then shut it again. She looked helplessly at Maggie.

And, unexpectedly, P.J. spoke up. "She told us she had to get the slaves free before Hunter Redfern had them all killed," she said in her light, strong child's voice. She was standing straight, her slender body drawn to its fullest height. Her blond hair shone pale above her small earnest face. Her words had the unmistakable ring of truth.

Something flashed in Jeanne's eyes. Her lip quirked, then she bit it. "She sure did. And I told her she was crazy."

"And in the beginning, when Jeanne showed her what they do to escaped slaves here, Maggie said it had to stop." P.J.'s voice was still clear and confident. "She said she couldn't let them *do* things like that to people."

"She said *we* couldn't let them do things like that," Jeanne corrected. "And she was crazy again. There's no way to stop them."

Laundress stared at her for a moment, then turned her burning gaze on Maggie. Her eyes were so fierce that Maggie was afraid she was going to attack. Then, all at once, she thrust the knife back in her pocket.

"Blasphemer!" she said harshly to Jeanne. "Don't talk about the Deliverer that way! Do you want to take away our only hope?"

Jeanne raised an eyebrow. "*You* were the one about to take it away," she pointed out.

Laundress glared at her. Then she turned to Maggie and a change came over her gaunt features. It wasn't much; they still remained as severe and grim as ever, but there was something like a bleak smile twisting her mouth.

"If you are the Deliverer," she said, "you've got your work cut out for you."

"Just everybody hang on one second," Maggie said.

Her head was whirling. She understood what was going on—sort of. These people believed she was some legendary figure come to save them. Because of a prophecy—they seemed to have a lot of prophecies around here.

But she couldn't really be their Deliverer. She *knew* that. She was just an ordinary girl. And hadn't anybody else ever worn a flowered top in this place?

Well—maybe not. Not a slave anyway. Maggie looked at Laundress's clothes again with new eyes. If they all wore this sort of thing, hand sewn and plain as a burlap sack, maybe a machine-made top with bright colors and a little wilted lace *would* look like something from a legend.

And I bet nobody wears red and blue socks, she thought and almost smiled. Especially at once.

She remembered how Sylvia had looked at them. Normally she would have been terribly embarrassed by that, perfect Sylvia looking at her imperfections. But the socks had been what started her on this whole journey by convincing her that Sylvia was lying. And just now they'd saved her life. If Laundress had attacked Jeanne or Cady, Maggie would have had to fight her.

But I'm still not the Deliverer, she thought. I have to explain that to them. . . .

"And since she's the Deliverer, you're going to help us, right?" Jeanne was saying. "You're going to heal Cady and feed us and hide us and everything? And help Maggie find out what happened to her brother?"

Maggie blinked, then grimaced. She could see Jeanne looking at her meaningfully. She shut her mouth.

"I'll help you any way I can," Laundress said. "But you'd better do your part. Do you have a plan, Deliverer?"

Maggie rubbed her forehead. Things were happening very fast—but even if she wasn't the Deliverer, she *had* come to help the slaves get free. Maybe it didn't matter what they called her.

She looked at Cady again, then at Jeanne, and at P.J., who was staring at her with shining confidence in her young eyes. Then she looked at the girl named Soaker, who was wearing the same expression.

Finally she looked into the gaunt, hard-bitten face of Laundress. There was no easy confidence here, but there was that half-stifled look of hope deep in the burning gaze.

"I don't have a plan yet," she said. "But I'll come up with one. And I don't know if I can really help you people. But I'll try."

CHAPTER 14

Maggie woke up slowly and almost luxuriously. She wasn't freezing. She wasn't aching or weak with hunger. And she had an unreasonable feeling of safety. Then she sat up and the safe feeling disappeared.

She was in Laundress's hut of earth bricks. Jeanne and P.J. were there, but Cady had been taken to another hut to be treated. Laundress had stayed all night with her, and Maggie had no idea if she was getting better or not. The frightened girl called Soaker brought them breakfast, but could only say that Cady was still asleep.

Breakfast was the same as dinner last night had been: a sort of thick oatmeal sweetened with huckleberries. Maggie ate it gratefully. It was good—at least to somebody as hungry as she was.

"We're lucky to have it," Jeanne said, stretching. She and P.J. were sitting opposite Maggie on the bare earth of the floor, eating with their fingers. They all were wearing the coarse, scratchy tunics and loose leggings of slaves, and Maggie kept going into spasms of twitching when the material made her itch somewhere she couldn't reach. Maggie's clothes, including her precious socks, were hidden at the back of the hut.

"They don't grow much grain or vegetable stuff," Jeanne was saying. "And of course slaves don't get to eat any meat. Only the vampires and the shapeshifters get to eat blood or flesh."

P.J. shivered, hunching up her thin shoulders. "When you say it like that, it makes me not *want* to eat it."

Jeanne gave a sharp-toothed grin. "They're afraid it would make the slaves too strong. Everything here's designed for that. Maybe you noticed, there's not much in the slave quarters made of wood."

Maggie blinked. She *had* noticed that vaguely, at the back of her mind. The huts were made of bricks, with hard-packed dirt floors. And there were no wooden tools like rakes or brooms lying around.

"But what do they burn?" she asked, looking at the small stone hearth built right on the floor of the hut. There was a hole in the roof above to let smoke out.

"Charcoaled wood, cut in little pieces. They make it out in the forest in charcoal pits, and it's strictly regulated. Everybody only gets so much. If they find a slave with extra wood, they execute 'em."

"Because wood kills vampires," Maggie said.

Jeanne nodded. "And silver kills shapeshifters. Slaves are forbidden to have silver, too—not that any of them are likely to get hold of any."

P.J. was looking out the small window of the hut. There was no glass in it, and last night it had been stuffed with sacking against the cold air. "If slaves can't eat meat, what are those?" she asked.

Maggie leaned to look. Outside two big calves were tethered to iron pickets. There were also a dozen trussed-up chickens and a pig in a pen made of rope.

"Those are for Night People," Jeanne said. "The shapeshifters and witches eat regular food—and so do the vampires, when they want to. It looks like they're going to have a feast—they don't bring the animals here until they're ready to slaughter."

P.J.'s face was troubled. "I feel sorry for them," she said softly.

"Yeah, well, there are worse things than being hit over the head," Jeanne said. "See those cages just beyond the pig? That's where the exotics are—the tigers and things they bring in to hunt. *That's* a bad way to die."

Maggie felt ice down her spine. "Let's hope we never have to find out—" she was beginning, when a flash of movement outside caught her eye.

"Get down!" she said sharply, and ducked out of the line of

sight of the window. Then, very carefully, with her body tense, she edged up to the open square again and peered out.

"What is it?" Jeanne hissed. P.J. just cowered on the floor, breathing quickly.

Maggie whispered, "Sylvia."

Two figures had appeared, walking through the back court-yard and talking as they went. Sylvia and Gavin. Sylvia's gown today was misty leaf green, and her hair rippled in shimmering waves over her shoulders. She looked beautiful and graceful and fragile.

"Are they coming here?" Jeanne breathed.

Maggie shook a hand—held low to the ground—toward her to be quiet. She was afraid of the same thing. If the Night People began a systematic search of the huts, they were lost.

But instead, Sylvia turned toward the cages that held the exotics. She seemed to be looking at the animals, occasionally turning to make a remark to Gavin.

"Now, what's she up to?" a voice murmured by Maggie's ear. Jeanne had crept up beside her.

"I don't know. Nothing good," Maggie whispered.

"They must be planning a hunt," Jeanne said grimly. "That's bad. I heard they were going to do a big one when Delos came to an agreement with Hunter Redfern."

Maggie drew in her breath. Had things gone that far already? It meant she didn't have much time left.

Outside, she could see Sylvia shaking her head, then

moving on to the pens and tethers holding the domestic animals.

"Get back," Maggie whispered, ducking down. But Sylvia never looked at the hut. She made some remark while looking at the calves and smiling. Then she and Gavin turned and strolled back through the kitchen garden.

Maggie watched until they were out of sight, chewing her lip. Then she looked at Jeanne.

"I think we'd better go see Laundress."

The hut Jeanne led her to was a little bigger than the others and had what Maggie knew by now was an amazing luxury: two rooms. Cady was in the tiny room—hardly bigger than an alcove—in back.

And she was looking better. Maggie saw it immediately. The clammy, feverish look was gone and so were the blue-black shadows under her eyes. Her breathing was deep and regular and her lashes lay heavy and still on her smooth cheeks.

"Is she going to be all right?" Maggie asked Laundress eagerly.

The gaunt woman was sponging Cady's cheeks with a cloth. Maggie was surprised at how tender the big red-knuckled hands could be.

"She'll live as long as any of us," Laundress said grimly, and Jeanne gave a wry snort. Even Maggie felt her lip twitch. She was beginning to like this woman. In fact, if Jeanne and

Laundress were examples, the slaves here had a courage and a black humor that she couldn't help but admire.

"I had a daughter," Laundress said. "She was about this one's age, but she had that one's coloring." She nodded slightly at P.J., who clutched at the baseball cap stashed inside her tunic and smiled.

Maggie hesitated, then asked. "What happened to her?"

"One of the nobles saw her and liked her," Laundress said. She wrung out the cloth and put it down, then stood briskly. When she saw Maggie still looking at her, she added, as if she were talking about the weather, "He was a shapeshifter, a wolf named Autolykos. He bit her and passed his curse on to her, but then he got tired of her. One night he made her run and hunted her down."

Maggie's knees felt weak. She couldn't think of anything to say that wouldn't be colossally stupid, so she didn't say anything.

P.J. did. "I'm sorry," she said in a husky little voice, and she put her small hand in Laundress's rough one.

Laundress touched the top of the shaggy blond head as if she were touching an angel.

"Um, can I talk to her? Cady?" Maggie asked, blinking fast and clearing her throat.

Laundress looked at her sharply. "No. You won't be able to wake her up. I had to give her strong medicine to fight off what *they'd* given her. You know how the potion works."

Maggie shook her head. "What potion?"

"They gave her calamus and bloodwort—and other things. It was a truth potion."

"You mean they wanted to get information out of her?"

Laundress only dignified that with a bare nod for an answer.

"But I wonder why?" Maggie looked at Jeanne, who shrugged.

"She's a witch from Outside. Maybe they thought she knew something."

Maggie considered another minute, then gave it up. She would just have to ask Cady when Cady was awake.

"There was another reason I wanted to see you," she said to Laundress, who was now briskly cleaning up the room. "Actually, a couple of reasons. I wanted to ask you about this."

She reached inside her slave tunic and pulled out the photo of Miles that she'd taken from her jacket last night.

"Have you seen him?"

Laundress took the picture between a callused thumb and forefinger and looked at it warily. "Wonderfully small painting," she said.

"It's called a photograph. It's not exactly painted." Maggie was watching the woman's face, afraid to hope.

There was no sign of recognition. "He's related to you," Laundress said, holding the photo to Maggie.

"He's my brother. From Outside, you know? And his girlfriend was Sylvia Weald. He disappeared last week."

"Witch Sylvia!" a cracked, shaky voice said.

Maggie looked up fast. There was an old woman in the doorway, a tiny, wizened creature with thin white hair and a face exactly like one of the dried-apple dolls Maggie had seen at fairs.

"This is Old Mender," Jeanne said. "She sews up torn clothes, you know? And she's the other healing woman."

"So this is the Deliverer," the cracked voice said, and the woman shuffled closer, peering at Maggie. "She looks like an ordinary girl, until you see the eyes."

Maggie blinked. "Oh—thanks," she said. Secretly she thought that Old Mender herself looked more like a witch than anyone she'd ever seen in her life. But there was bright intelligence in the old woman's birdlike gaze and her little smile was sweet.

"Witch Sylvia came to the castle a week ago," she told Maggie, her head on one side. "She didn't have any boy with her, but she was talking about a boy. My grand-nephew Currier heard her. She was telling Prince Delos how she'd chosen a human for a plaything, and she'd tried to bring him to the castle for Samhain. But the boy did something—turned on her somehow. And so she had to punish him, and that had delayed her."

Maggie's heart was beating in her ears. "Punish him," she began, and then she said, "What's Samhain?"

"Halloween," Jeanne said. "The witches here normally have a big celebration at midnight."

Halloween. All right. Maggie's mind was whirring desperately, ticking over this new information. So now she knew for certain that Sylvia *had* gone hiking on Halloween with Miles, just as she'd told the sheriffs and rangers. Or maybe they'd been driving, if Jeanne's story about a mysterious pass that only Night People could see was true. But anyway they'd been coming here, to the Dark Kingdom. And something had delayed them. Miles had done something that made Sylvia terribly angry and changed her mind about taking him to the castle.

And made her . . . punish him. In some way that Maggie wasn't supposed to be able to guess.

Maybe she just killed him after all, Maggie thought, with an awful sinking in her stomach. She could have shoved him off a cliff easily. Whatever she did, he never made it here—right?

"So there isn't any human boy in the dungeon or anything?" she asked, looking at Laundress and then Mender. But she knew the answer before they shook their heads.

Nobody recognizes him. He can't be here.

Maggie felt her shoulders slump. But although she was discouraged and heartsick, she wasn't defeated. What she felt instead was a hard little burning like a coal in her chest. She wanted more than ever to grab Sylvia and shake the truth out of her.

At the very least, if nothing else, I'm going to find out how he died. Because that's important.

Funny how it didn't seem impossible anymore that Miles *was* dead. Maggie had learned a lot since coming to this valley. People got hurt and died and had other awful things happen to them, and that was that. The ones left alive had to find some way of going on.

But not of forgetting.

"You said you had two reasons for coming to see me," Laundress prompted. She was standing with her big hands on her hips, her gaunt body erect and looking just slightly impatient. "Have you come up with a plan, Deliverer?"

"Well—sort of. Not exactly a *plan* so much as—well, I guess it's a plan." Maggie floundered, trying to explain herself. The truth was that she'd come up with the most basic plan of all.

To go see Delos.

That was it. The simplest, most direct solution. She was going to get him alone and talk to him. Use the weird connection between them if she had to. Pound some sort of understanding into his thick head.

And put her life on the line to back up her words.

Jeanne thought the slaves were going to be killed when Hunter Redfern and Delos made their deal. Maggie was a slave now. If the other slaves were killed, Maggie would be with them.

And you're betting that he'll *care*, a nasty little voice in her brain whispered. But you don't really know that. He keeps threatening to kill you himself. He specifically warned you not to come to the castle.

Well, anyway, we're going to find out, Maggie told the little voice. And if I can't convince him, I'll have to do something more violent.

"I need to get into the castle," she said to Laundress. "Not just into the kitchen, you know, but the other rooms—wherever I might be able to find Prince Delos alone."

"Alone? You won't find him alone anywhere but his bedchamber."

"Well, then, I have to go there."

Laundress was watching her narrowly. "Is it assassination you've got in mind? Because I know someone who has a piece of wood."

"It . . ." Maggie stopped and took a breath. "I really hope it isn't going to come to that. But maybe I'd better take the wood, just in case."

And you'd better hope for a miracle, the nasty voice in her mind said. Because how else are you going to overpower him?

Jeanne was rubbing her forehead. When she spoke, Maggie knew she'd been thinking along the same lines. "Look, dummy, are you sure this is a good idea? I mean, he's—"

"A Night Person," Maggie supplied.

"And you're—"

"Just an ordinary human."

"She's the Deliverer," P.J. said stoutly, and Maggie paused to smile at her.

Then she turned back to Jeanne. "I don't know if it's a good idea, but it's my only idea. And I know it's dangerous, but I have to do it." She looked awkwardly at Laundress and Old Mender. "The truth is that it's not just about you people here. If what Jeanne told you about Hunter Redfern is right, then the whole human world is in trouble."

"Oh, the prophecies," Old Mender said, and cackled.

"You know them, too?"

"We slaves hear everything." Old Mender smiled and nodded. "Especially when it concerns our own prince. I remember when he was little—I was the Queen's seamstress then, before she died. His mother knew the prophecies, and she said,

"In blue fire, the final darkness is banished.
In blood, the final price is paid."

Blood, Maggie thought. She knew that blood had to run before Delos could use the blue fire, but this sounded as if it were talking about something darker. Whose blood? she wondered.

"And the final darkness is the end of the world, right?" she said. "So you can see how important it is for me to change Delos's mind. Not just for the slaves, but for all humans." She looked at Jeanne as she spoke. Laundress and

Old Mender didn't know anything about the world Outside, but Jeanne did.

Jeanne gave a sort of grudging nod, to say that, yeah, putting off the end of the world was important. "Okay, so we have to try it. We'd better find out which slaves are allowed in his room, and then we can go up and hide. The big chambers have wardrobes, right?" She was looking at Old Mender, who nodded. "We can stay in one of those—"

"That's a good idea," Maggie interrupted. "Everything but the we. You can't go with me this time. This is something I have to do alone."

Jeanne gave an indignant wriggle of her shoulders. Her red hair seemed to stand up in protest and her eyes were sparking. "That's ridiculous. I can help. There's no reason—"

"There is, too, a reason," Maggie said. "It's too danger-ous. Whoever goes there might get killed today. If you stay here, you may at least have a few more days." When Jeanne opened her mouth to protest, she went on, "Days to try and figure out a new plan, okay? Which will probably be just as dangerous. And, besides, I'd like somebody to watch over P.J. and Cady for as long as possible." She gave P.J. a smile, and P.J. lifted her head resolutely, obviously trying to stop her chin from quivering.

"I really do need to do it alone," Maggie said gently, turn-ing back to Jeanne. Somewhere in her own mind, she was standing back, astonished. Who would have ever thought, when she first met Jeanne in the cart, that she would end up having to talk her out of trying to get killed with Maggie?

Jeanne blew air out pursed lips, her eyes narrowed. Finally she nodded.

"Fine, fine. You go conquer the vampire and I'll stay and arrange the revolution."

"I bet you will," Maggie said dryly. For a moment their eyes met, and it was like that first time, when an unspoken bond had formed between them.

"*Try* to take care of yourself. You're not exactly the smartest, you know," Jeanne said. Her voice was a little rough and her eyes were oddly shiny.

"I know," Maggie said.

The next moment Jeanne sniffed and cheered up. "I just thought of who's allowed up into the bedrooms in the morning," she said. "You can help her, and she'll lead you to Delos's room."

Maggie looked at her suspiciously. "Why are you so happy about it? Who is it?"

"Oh, you'll like her. She's called Chamber-pot Emptier."

CHAPTER 15

Maggie shuffled behind Chamber-pot Emptier, heading back toward the castle. She was carrying piles of folded linen sheets given to her by Laundress, and she was doing her best to look like a slave. Laundress had smudged her face artistically with dirt to disguise her. She had also sifted a handful of dust into Maggie's hair to dull the auburn into a lifeless brown, and when Maggie bowed her head over the sheets, the hair further obscured her features. The only problem was that she was constantly afraid she was going to sneeze.

"Those are the wild animals," Chamber-pot Emptier whispered over her shoulder. She was a big-boned girl with gentle eyes that reminded Maggie of the calves tethered by Laundress's hut. It had taken Laundress a while to make her understand what they wanted of her, but now she seemed to feel obligated to give Maggie a tour.

"They're brought in from Outside," she said. "And they're dangerous."

Maggie looked sideways at the wicker cages where Sylvia and Gavin had walked earlier. From one a brown-gray wolf stared back at her with a frighteningly sad and steady gaze. In another a sleek black panther was pacing, and it snarled as they went by. There was something curled up in the back of a third that might have been a tiger—it was big, and it had stripes.

"Wow," she said. "I wouldn't want to chase that."

Chamber-pot Emptier seemed pleased. "And here's the castle. It's called Black Dawn."

"It is?" Maggie said, distracted away from the animals.

"That's what my grandpa called it, anyway. He lived and died in the courtyard without ever going in." Chamber-pot Emptier thought a moment and added, "The old people say that you used to be able to see the sun in the sky—not just behind the clouds, you know. And when the sun came up in the morning it shone on the castle. But maybe that's just a story."

Yeah, maybe it was just a story that you could see the sun in the sky, Maggie thought grimly. Every time she thought this place couldn't surprise her anymore, she discovered she was wrong.

But the castle itself was impressive . . . awe inspiring. It was the only thing in view that wasn't dusty brown or pallid gray. Its walls were shiny and black, almost mirrorlike in places, and

Maggie didn't have to be told that it wasn't built of any ordinary human stone. How they had gotten it to this valley was a mystery.

Delos lives here, she thought as Emptier led her up a stone staircase, past the ground floor, which was just cellars and storage rooms. In this beautiful, frightening, impressive place. Not only lives in it, but commands it. It's all his.

She got just a glimpse of the great hall, where she'd seen slaves setting a long table yesterday. Chamber-pot Emptier led her up another floor and into a series of winding corridors that seemed to go on for miles.

It was dim in this internal labyrinth. The windows were high and narrow and hardly let any of the pale daylight in. On the walls there were candles in brackets and flares in iron rings, but they only seemed to add wavering, confusing shadows to the twilight.

"His bedroom's up here," Emptier murmured finally. Maggie followed her closely. She was just thinking that they had made it all the way without even being challenged, when a voice sounded from a side corridor.

"Where are you going? Who's this?"

It was a guard, Maggie saw, peering from under her hair. A real medieval guard, with, of all things, a lance. There was another one in the opposite corridor just like him. She was fascinated in the middle of her terror.

But Chamber-pot Emptier of the not-so-quick wits reacted

beautifully. She took time to curtsey, then she said slowly and stolidly, "It's Folder from the laundry, sir. Laundress sent her with the sheets and I was told she could help me. There's more work because of the guests, you know."

"It's Chamber Maid's work to spread sheets," the guard said irritably.

Chamber-pot Emptier curtsied again and said just as slowly, "Yes, sir, but there's more work because of the guests, you see—"

"Fine, fine," the guard broke in impatiently, "Why don't you go and do it, instead of talking about it?" He seemed to think that was funny, and he turned and elbowed the other guard in the ribs.

Chamber-pot Emptier curtseyed a third time and walked on, not hurrying. Maggie tried to copy the curtsey, with her face buried in the sheets.

There was another endless corridor, then a doorway, and then Emptier said, "We're here. And there's nobody around."

Maggie lifted her face from the sheets. "You're absolutely wonderful, you know that? You deserve an Academy Award."

"A what?"

"Never mind. But you were great."

"I only told the truth," the girl said placidly, but there was a smile lurking in the depths of her gentle cowlike eyes. "There is more work when guests come. We never had them before three years ago."

Maggie nodded. "I know. Look, I guess you'd better go now. And um—Emptier?" She couldn't bring herself to say the entire name. "I really hope you don't get in trouble because of this."

Chamber-pot Emptier nodded back, then went to reach under the bed and retrieve a ceramic container. She walked out again holding it carefully.

Maggie looked around the room, which was very big and very bare. It was somewhat better lit than the corridors, having several bowl-shaped oil lamps on stands. The bed was the only real piece of furniture in it. It was huge, with a heavy wooden frame and carved bedposts. Piled on top of it were quilts and what looked like fur coverlets, and hanging all around it were linen curtains.

I'm probably supposed to take all that stuff off and put the clean sheets on, Maggie thought. She didn't.

The rest of the furniture seemed to be large chests made of exotic-looking wood, and a few benches and stools. Nothing that offered a hiding place. But on one side there was a curtained doorway.

Maggie went through it and found a small anteroom— the wardrobe Jeanne had mentioned. It was much bigger than she'd expected, and seemed to be more of a storeroom than a closet.

Okay. So I'll just sit down.

There were two stools beside a figure that vaguely resembled a dressmaker's dummy. Maggie dropped her sheets on a chest and pulled one of the stools close to the doorway. Through the space between the linen curtains she could see almost the entire bedchamber.

Perfect, she thought. All I have to do is wait until he comes in alone. And then—

She stiffened. She could hear voices from somewhere beyond the vast bedroom. No, she could hear *a* voice, a musical girlish voice.

Oh, please, she thought. Not *her*. Don't let him come in with her. I'll have to jump out and hit her with something; I won't be able to stop myself. . . .

But when two figures came in the room, she had no desire to jump out.

It was Sylvia, all right, but she wasn't with Delos. She was with Hunter Redfern.

Maggie felt ice down her spine. Now, what were these two doing in Delos's bedroom? Whatever it was, if they caught her, she was dead meat. She held herself absolutely still, but she couldn't tear herself away from the curtain.

"He's out riding, and he won't be back for another half hour," Sylvia was saying. She was wearing a dark holly-green gown and carrying a basket. "And I've sent all the servants away."

"Even so," Hunter Redfern said. He gently moved the heavy wooden door until it was almost shut. Not all the way, but enough to screen the bedchamber from anyone outside.

"You really think he's spying on our rooms?" Sylvia turned in a swirl of skirts to look at the tall man.

"He's bright—much smarter than you give him credit for. And these old castles have spy-holes and listening tubes built in; I remember. It's a stupid prince who doesn't make use of them."

He remembers, Maggie thought, for a moment too full of wonder to be scared. He remembers the days when castles were built, he means. He's really been alive that long.

She studied the handsome face under the blood-red hair, the aristocratic cheekbones, the mobile mouth—and the quick flashing eyes. This was the sort of man who could fascinate people, she decided. Like Delos, there was a sort of leashed tension about him, a reserve of power and intelligence that made an ordinary person feel awed. He was a leader, a commander.

And a hunter, Maggie thought. All these people are hunters, but he's *the* Hunter, the epitome of what they are. His name says it all.

But Sylvia was talking again. "What is it that he's not supposed to know?"

"I've had a message from Outside. Don't ask how, I have my ways."

"You have your little bats," Sylvia said demurely. "I've seen them."

There was a pause, then Hunter said, "You'd better watch yourself, girl. That mouth's going to get you in trouble."

Sylvia had her face turned away from him, but Maggie saw her swallow. "I'm sorry. I didn't know it was a secret. But what's happened?"

"The biggest news in your short life." Hunter Redfern laughed once and added with apparent good humor restored, "And maybe in mine. The witches have seceded from the Night World."

Maggie blinked. It sounded impressive the way he said it—but more impressive was the way Sylvia froze and then whirled breathlessly.

"What?"

"It's happened. They've been threatening for a month, but most people didn't believe they'd really do it."

Sylvia put a hand to her middle, pressed flat against her stomach as if to hold something in. Then she sat on the fur-covered bed.

"They've left the Council," she said. She wasn't looking at Hunter Redfern.

"They've left the Council and everything else."

"All of them?"

Hunter Redfern's fine red eyebrows went up. "What did you expect? Oh, a few of the blackest practitioners from Circle Midnight are arguing, but most of them agree with the liberals in Circle Twilight. They want to save the humans. Avert the coming darkness." He said it exactly the way Maggie had heard lumberjacks say, "Save the spotted owls. Ha!"

"So it's really beginning," Sylvia murmured. She was still looking at the stone floor. "I mean, there's no going back now, is there? The Night World is split forever."

"And the millennium is upon us," Hunter said, almost cheerfully. He looked young and . . . personable, Maggie thought. Somebody you'd vote for.

"Which brings me to the question," he said smoothly, looking at Sylvia, "of when you're going to find her."

What her? Maggie's stomach tightened.

Sylvia's face was equally tight. She looked up and said levelly, "I told you I'd find her and I will."

"But *when*? You do understand how important this is?"

"Of course I understand!" Sylvia flared up. Her chest was heaving. "That's why I was trying to send her to you in the first place—"

Hunter was talking as if he didn't hear her. "If it gets out that Aradia, the Maiden of all the witches, is here in the valley—"

"I know!"

"And that you *had* her and let her slip through your fingers—"

"I was trying to bring her to *you*. I thought *that* was important," Sylvia said. She was bristling and distraught. Which was exactly what Hunter wanted her to be, Maggie thought dazedly. He really knows how to play people.

But the analysis was faraway, in the shallowest part of her mind. Most of her consciousness was simply stricken into paralyzed amazement.

Aradia.

The Maiden of all the witches.

So it wasn't Arcadia at all, Maggie thought. She might have mentioned *that*, after I've been calling her Cady for days. But then she hasn't been conscious much, and when she was we had more urgent things to talk about.

Aradia. Aradia. That's really pretty.

The name had started an odd resonance in her mind, maybe bringing up some long-forgotten mythology lesson. Aradia was a goddess, she thought. Of . . . um, sylvan glades or something. The woods. Like Diana.

And what Maiden of all the witches was, she had no idea, but it was obviously something important. And not evil, either. From what Hunter was saying, it was clear that witches weren't like other Night People.

She was the maiden Bern and Gavin were talking about, Maggie realized. The one they were supposed to deliver. So Sylvia was bringing her to Hunter Redfern. But Cady herself told me—I mean, *Aradia* told me—that she was already coming to this valley for a reason.

Before she could even properly phrase the question, her mind had the answer.

Delos.

In a coincidence that lifted the hair on Maggie's arms, Sylvia said, "She won't get to Delos."

"She'd better not," Hunter said, "Maybe you don't realize how persuasive she can be. An ambassador from all the witches, coming to plead her case . . . she just might sway him. He has a despicable soft spot—a conscience, you might call it. And we know he's been in contact with the human girl who escaped with her. Who knows what messages the little vermin was carrying from her?"

No messages, Maggie thought grimly. Not with this vermin anyway. But I would have carried them if I'd known.

"Gavin said Aradia was still unconscious from the truth potion—that she was practically dead," Sylvia said. "I don't think she could have given any messages. I'd swear that Delos doesn't know she's in the valley at all."

Hunter was still brooding. "The witches have one Wild Power on their side already."

"But they won't get another," Sylvia said doggedly. "I've got people looking for her. All the nobles are on our side. They won't let her get to Delos."

"She should have been killed in the beginning," Hunter mused. "But maybe *you* have a soft spot for her—like you do for that human boy."

Behind the linen curtains, Maggie stiffened.

Like you *do*. Not like you *did*. And who else could the human boy be?

She gritted her teeth, listening so hard she could hear the blood in her ears, willing them to talk about Miles.

But Hunter was going on in his smooth voice, "Or maybe you still have some loyalty to the witches."

Sylvia's pale face flushed. "I do not! I'm finished with them, and you know it! I may be a spellcaster, but I'm not a witch anymore."

"It's good to see you haven't forgotten what they've done to you," Hunter said. "After all, you could have been a Hearth-Woman, taken your rightful place on the witch Council."

"Yes . . ."

"Like your grandmother and her mother before her. *They* were Harmans, and so was your father. What a pity the name isn't passed through the male line. You ended up being just a Weald."

"I *was* a Harman," Sylvia said with muted ferocity. She was staring at the floor again, and she seemed to be speaking to herself rather than to Hunter. "I *was*. But I had to stand there and watch my cousins be accepted instead of me. I had to watch *half humans* be accepted—be welcomed. They took my place—just because they were descended through the female line."

Hunter shook his head. "A very sad tradition."

Sylvia's breath came raggedly for another minute or so, then she looked up slowly at the tall man in the center of the room. "You don't have to worry about my loyalty," she said quietly. "I want a place in the new order after the millennium. I'm through with the witches."

Hunter smiled.

"I know it," he said, lightly and approvingly, and then he started pacing the room. He got what he wanted out of her, Maggie thought.

Almost casually, he added, "Just be sure that Delos's power is kept in check until everything's decided."

Sylvia bent and lifted the basket, which Maggie had forgotten about.

"The new binding spells will hold," she said. "I brought special ingredients from one of the oldest Midnight witches. And he won't suspect anything."

"And nobody but you can take them off?"

"Nobody but me," Sylvia said firmly. "Not even the Crone of all the witches. Or the Maiden, for that matter."

"Good girl," Hunter said, and smiled again. "I have every confidence in you. After all, you have lamia blood in you to balance the witch taint. You're my own eighth-great-granddaughter."

Maggie wanted to punch him.

She was confused and frightened and indignant and furious, all at once. As far as she could tell, Hunter Redfern seemed to be manipulating everybody. And Delos, Delos the prince and Wild Power, was just another of his puppets.

I wonder what they plan to do if he *won't* join their new order? she thought bleakly.

After a few minutes, Hunter turned in his pacing and walked by the door. He paused briefly as if listening, then glanced at Sylvia.

"You don't know how happy it makes me just to think about it," he said, in a voice that wasn't strained, or overly cheerful, or too loud, or anything that rang false. "To finally have a true heir. A male heir of my own line, and untainted by witch blood. I would never have married that witch Maeve Harman if I had known my son was still alive. And not only alive, but out having sons! The only true Redferns left in the world, you might say."

Maggie, with her teeth set in her lower lip, didn't need to guess who was on the other side of the door. She watched tensely.

And Delos came in, right on cue.

CHAPTER 16

I'm sorry. Was I interrupting something?" he said.

Maggie had to struggle not to draw in her breath sharply.

It was always a little bit of a shock seeing him. And even in a room with Hunter Redfern and the pale and dazzling Sylvia, he stood out. Like a cold wind blowing through the door, he seemed to bring coiled energy in with him, to slap everyone awake with the chilly smell of snow.

And of course he was gorgeous, too.

And not awed by Hunter, Maggie thought. He faced his great-grandfather with those fearless yellow eyes level, and a measuring look on his fine-boned face.

"Nothing at all," Hunter Redfern said amiably. "We were waiting for you. And planning the celebrations."

"Celebrations?"

"To honor our agreement. I'm so pleased that we've come to an understanding at last. Aren't you?"

"Of course," Delos said, pulling off his gloves without any change in expression. "When we do come to an understanding, I'll be very pleased."

Maggie had to bite her lip on a snicker. At that moment, looking at Hunter's facile smile and Sylvia's pinned-on simper, she had never liked Delos's dour, cold grimness better.

Idiot, she told herself. When did you ever like it at all? The guy's an icicle.

But there was something clean and sharp-edged about his iciness, and she couldn't help admiring the way he faced Hunter. There was a little aching knot in her chest as she watched him standing there, tense and elegant, with his dark hair tousled from riding.

Which wasn't to say she wasn't scared. That aura of power Delos carried along with him was very real. He had sensed her before, even with Aradia blocking the signs of her life force. And now here he was, maybe twelve feet away, with only a piece of linen between them.

There was nothing Maggie could do but sit as still as possible.

"Sylvia has taken the liberty of beginning the preparations," Hunter said. "I hope you don't mind. I think we can work out any little details that are left before tomorrow, don't you?"

Suddenly Delos looked tired. He tossed his gloves on the bed and nodded, conceding a point. "Yes."

"Essentially," Hunter Redfern said, "we are agreed."

This time Delos just nodded without speaking.

"I can't wait to show you off to the world Outside," Hunter said, and this time Maggie thought the note of pride and eagerness in his voice was sincere. "My great-grandson. And to think that a year ago I didn't know of your existence." He crossed to slap Delos on the back. It was a gesture so much like the old king's that Maggie's eyes widened.

"I'm going to make some preparations of my own," he said. "I think the last hunt before you leave should be special, don't you?"

He was smiling as he left.

Delos stared moodily at the fur coverlet.

"Well," Sylvia said, sounding almost chirpy. "How's the arm?"

Delos glanced down at it. He was still wearing the complicated brace thing Maggie had seen him in yesterday.

"It's all right."

"Hurts?"

"A little."

Sylvia sighed and shook her head. "That's because you used it for practice. I did warn you, you know."

"Can you make it better or not?" Delos said brusquely.

Sylvia was already opening the basket. "I told you, it'll take time. But it should improve with each treatment—as long as you don't use it."

She was fiddling with the brace, doing things that Maggie couldn't see. And Maggie's heart was beating hard with anger and an unreasonable protectiveness.

I can't let her do that to Delos—but how can I stop her? There's no way. If she sees me, it's all over. . . .

"There," Sylvia said. "That should hold you for a while."

Maggie ground her teeth.

But at least maybe she'll go *now,* she thought. *It feels like about a century I've been sitting in here listening to her. And this stool isn't getting any more comfortable.*

"Now," Sylvia said briskly, tidying. "Just let me put your gloves away—"

Oh, no, Maggie thought, horrified. On the shelf beside her was a pile of gloves.

"No," Delos said, so quickly it was almost an echo. "I need them."

"Don't be silly. You're not going out again—"

"I'll take them." Delos had wonderful reflexes. He put himself between Sylvia and the wardrobe, and an instant later he was holding on to the gloves, almost tugging them from her hands.

Sylvia looked up at him wonderingly for a long moment. Maggie could see her face, the creamy skin delicately flushed, and her eyes, the color of tear-drenched violets. She could see the shimmer of her pale blond hair as Sylvia shook her head slightly.

Delos stared down at her implacably.

Then Sylvia shrugged her fragile shoulders and let go of the gloves.

"I'll go see to the feast," she said lightly and smiled. She picked up her basket and moved gracefully to the door.

Delos watched her go.

Maggie simply sat, speechless and paralyzed. When Delos followed Sylvia and closed the door firmly behind her, she made herself get slowly off the stool. She backed away from the curtains slightly, but she could still see a strip of the bedroom.

Delos walked unerringly straight to the wardrobe.

"You can come out now," he said, his voice flat and hard.

Maggie shut her eyes.

Great. Well, I should have known.

But he hadn't let Sylvia come in and discover her, and he hadn't simply turned her over to his guards. Those were very good signs, she told herself stoutly. In fact, maybe she wasn't going to have to persuade him of anything at all; maybe he was already going to be reasonable.

"Or do I have to come in?" Delos said dangerously.

Or maybe not, Maggie thought.

She felt a sudden idiotic desire to get the dust out of her hair. She shook her head a few times, brushing at it, then gave up.

Terribly conscious of her smudged face and slave clothing, she parted the linen hangings and walked out.

"I warned you," Delos said.

He was facing her squarely, his jaw set and his mouth as grim as she had ever seen it. His eyes were hooded, a dull and eerie gold in the shadows. He looked every inch the dark and mysterious vampire prince.

And here I am, Maggie thought. Looking like . . . well, like vermin, I bet. Like something fished out of the gutter. Not much of a representative for humanity.

She had never cared about clothes or hairstyles or things like that, but just now she wished that she could at least look presentable. Since the fate of the world might just depend on her.

Even so, there was something in the air between Delos and herself. A sort of quivering aliveness that quickened the blood in Maggie's veins. That stirred something in her chest, and started her heart pounding with an odd mixture of fear and hope.

She faced Delos just as squarely as he was facing her.

"I know some things that I think you need to know," she said quietly.

He ignored that. "I told you what would happen if you came here. I told you I wouldn't protect you again."

"I remember. But you *did* protect me again. And I thank you—but I really think I'd better tell you what's going on.

Sylvia is the suspicious type, and if she's gone to Hunter Redfern to say that you don't want people looking in your closet—"

"Don't you *understand*?" he said with such sudden violence that Maggie's throat closed, choking off her words. She stared at him. "You're so close to dying, but you don't seem to care. Are you too stupid to grasp it, or do you just have a death wish?"

The thumping in Maggie's chest now was definitely fear.

"I do understand," she began slowly, when she could get her voice to work.

"No, you *don't*," he said. "But I'll make you."

All at once his eyes were blazing. Not just their normal brilliant yellow, but a dazzling and unnatural gold that seemed to hold its own light.

Even though Maggie had seen it before, it was still a shock to watch his features change. His face going paler, even more beautiful and clearly defined, chiseled in ice. His pupils widening like a predator's, holding a darkness that a human could drown in. And that proud and willful mouth twisting in anger.

It all happened in a second or so. And then he was advancing on her, with dark fire in his eyes, and his lips pulling back from his teeth.

Maggie stared at the fangs, helplessly horrified all over again. They were even sharper than she remembered them looking. They indented his lower lip on either side, even with his mouth partly open. And, yes, they were definitely scary.

"This is what I am," Delos said, speaking easily around the fangs. "A hunting animal. Part of a world of darkness that you couldn't survive for a minute in. I've told you over and over to stay away from it, but you won't listen. You turn up *in my own castle*, and you just won't believe your danger. So now I'm going to show you."

Maggie took a step backward. She wasn't in a good position; the wall was behind her and the huge bed was on her left. Delos was between her and the door. And she had already seen how fast his reflexes were.

Her legs felt unsteady; her pulse was beating erratically. Her breath was coming fast.

He doesn't really mean it—he won't really do it. He isn't serious. . . .

But for all her mind's desperate chanting, panic was beginning to riot inside her. The instincts of forgotten ancestors, long buried, were surfacing. Some ancient part of her remembered being chased by hunting animals, being prey.

She backed up until she came in contact with the tapestry-hung wall behind her. And then there was nowhere else to go.

"Now," Delos said and closed the distance between them with the grace of a tiger.

He was right in front of her. Maggie couldn't help looking up at him, looking directly into that alien and beautiful face.

She could smell a scent like autumn leaves and fresh snow, but she could feel the heat from his body.

He's nothing dead or undead, some very distant part of her mind thought. He's ruthless, he's been raised to be a weapon, but he's definitely alive—maybe the most alive thing I've ever seen.

When he moved, there was nowhere she could go to avoid him. His hands closed on her shoulders like implacable bands of steel. And then he was pulling her forward, not roughly but not gently either, pulling her until her body rested lightly against his. And he was looking down at her with golden eyes that burned like twin flames.

Looking at my throat, Maggie thought. She could feel the pulse beating there, and with her chin tilted up to look at him and her upper body arched away from him, she knew he could see it. His eyes were fixed on it with a different kind of hunger than she had ever seen in a human face.

For just one instant the panic overwhelmed her, flooding up blackly to engulf everything else. She couldn't think; she was nothing but a terrified mass of instinct, and all she wanted to do was to *run*, to get away.

Then, slowly at first, the panic receded. It simply poured off her, draining away. She felt as if she were rising from deep water into air clear as crystal.

She looked straight into the golden eyes above her and said, "Go ahead."

She had the pleasure of seeing the golden eyes look startled. "What?"

"Go ahead," Maggie said distinctly. "It doesn't matter. You're stronger than me; we both know that. But whatever you do, you can't make me your prey. You don't have that power. You can't control me."

Delos hissed in fury, a reptilian sound. "You are so—"

"You wanted me scared; I'm scared. But, then, I was scared before. And it doesn't matter. There's something more important than me at stake here. Prove whatever you've got to prove and then I'll tell you about it."

"So completely stupid," Delos raged. But Maggie had the odd feeling that his anger was more against himself than her. "You don't think I'll hurt you," he said.

"You're wrong there."

"I *will* hurt you. I'll show you—"

"You can kill me," Maggie said clearly. "But that's all you can do. I told you, you can't control me. And you can't change what's between us."

He was very, very angry now. The fathomless pupils of his eyes were like black holes, and Maggie suddenly remembered that he wasn't just a vampire, or just a weapon, but some doomsday creature with powers meant for the end of the world.

He hovered over her with his fangs showing.

"I *will* hurt you," he said. "Watch me hurt you."

He bent to her angrily, and she could see his intent in his eyes. He meant to frighten and disillusion . . .

. . . and he kissed her mouth like raindrops falling on cool water.

Maggie clung to him desperately and kissed back. Where they touched they dissolved into each other.

Then she felt him tremble in her arms and they were both lost.

It was like the first time when their minds had joined. Maggie felt a pulsing thrill that enveloped her entire body. She could feel the pure line of communication open between them, she could feel herself lifted into that wonderful still place where only the two of them existed and nothing else mattered.

Dimly, she knew that her physical self was falling forward, that they were both falling, still clasped in each other's arms. But in the hushed place of crystalline beauty where she *really* was, they were facing each other in a white light.

It was like being inside his mind again, but this time he was there opposite her, gazing at her directly. He didn't look like a doomsday weapon anymore, or even like a vampire. His black-lashed golden eyes were large, like a solemn child's. There was a terrible wistfulness in his face.

He swallowed, and then she heard his mental voice. It was just the barest breath of sound. *I don't want this—*

Yes, you do, she interrupted, indignant. The normal barriers that existed between two people had melted; she knew what he was feeling, and she didn't like being lied to.

—to end, he finished.

Oh.

Maggie's eyes filled with sudden hot tears.

She did what was instinctive to her. She reached out to him. And then they were embracing in their minds, just as their physical bodies embraced, and there was that feeling of invisible wings all around them.

Maggie could catch fragments of his thoughts, not just the surface ones, but things so deep she wasn't sure he even knew he was thinking them. *So lonely . . . always been lonely. Meant to be that way. Always alone . . .*

No, you're not, she told him, trying to communicate it to the deepest part of him. *I won't let you be alone. And we were meant to be like this; can't you feel it?*

What she could feel was his powerful longing. But he couldn't be convinced all at once.

She heard something like *Destiny . . .* And she saw images of his past. His father. His teachers. The nobles. Even the slaves who had heard the prophecies. They all believed he had only one purpose, and it had to do with the end of the world.

You can change your destiny, she said. *You don't have to go along with it. I don't know what's going to happen with the world, but you don't have to be what they say. You have the power to fight them!*

For one heartbeat the image of his father seemed to loom closer, tall and terrible, a father seen through the eyes of childhood. Then the features blurred, changing just enough to become Hunter Redfern with the same cruel and accusing light in his yellow eyes.

And then the picture was swept away by a tidal wave of anger from Delos.

I am not a weapon.

I know that, Maggie told him.

I can choose what I am from now on. I can choose what path to follow.

Yes, Maggie said.

Delos said simply, *I choose to go with you.*

His anger was gone. Just briefly, she got the flicker of another image from him, as she had once before seeing herself through his eyes.

He didn't see her as a slave girl with dusty hair and a smudged face and coarse sacking for clothes. He saw her as the girl with autumn-colored hair and endlessly deep sorrel eyes—the kind of eyes that never wavered, but looked straight into his soul. He saw her as warm and real and vibrant, melting the black ice of his heart and setting him free.

And then this image was gone, too, and they were simply holding on to each other, lapped in peace.

They stayed like that for a while, their spirits flowing in and out of each other. Delos didn't seem inclined to move.

And Maggie wanted it to last, too. She wanted to stay here for a long time, exploring all the deepest and most secret places of the mind that was now open to her. To touch him in ways he'd never been touched before, this person who, beyond all logic, was the other half of her. Who belonged to her. Who was her soulmate.

But there was something nagging at her consciousness. She couldn't ignore it, and when she finally allowed herself to look at it, she remembered everything.

And she was swept with a wave of alarm so strong it snapped her right out of Delos's mind.

She could feel the shock of separation reverberate in him as she sat up, aware of her own body again. They were still linked enough that it hurt her just as it hurt him. But she was too frightened to care.

"Delos," she said urgently. "We've got to do something. There's going to be trouble."

He blinked at her, as if he were coming from very far away. "It will be all right," he said.

"No. It won't. You don't understand."

He sighed, very nearly his old exasperated snort. "If it's Hunter Redfern you're worried about—"

"It's him—and Sylvia. Delos, I heard them talking when I was in the wardrobe. You don't know what they've got planned."

"It doesn't matter what they've got planned. I can take

care of them." He straightened a little, looked down at his left arm.

"No, you can't," Maggie said fiercely. "And that's the problem. Sylvia put a spell on you, a binding spell, she called it. You can't use your power."

CHAPTER 17

He stared at her for an instant, his golden eyes wide. "Don't you believe me?"

"I wouldn't put it past Sylvia to try," he said. "But I don't think she's strong enough."

"She said she got special ingredients. And she said that nobody else could take the spell off." When he still looked doubtful, although a bit more grim, Maggie added, "Why don't you try it?"

He reached down with long, strong fingers to pull at the fastenings of his brace. It came off easily, and Maggie's eyebrows went up. She blinked.

He extended his arm, pointing it at the wall, and drew a dagger from his belt.

Maggie had forgotten about the blood part. She bit the inside of her cheek and didn't say anything as he opened a small cut on his wrist. Blood welled up red, then flowed in a trickle.

"Just a little blast," Delos said, and looked calmly at the wall. Nothing happened.

He frowned, his golden eyes flaring dangerously. Maggie could see the concentration in his face. He spread his fingers.

Still nothing happened.

Maggie let out her breath. I guess spells are invisible, she thought. The brace was just for show.

Delos was looking at his arm as if it didn't belong to him.

"We're in trouble," Maggie said, trying not to make it sound like *I told you so.* "While they thought they were alone in here, they were talking about all kinds of things. All Hunter cares about is getting you to help him destroy the humans. But there's been some big split in the Night World, and the witches have seceded from it."

Delos went very still, and his eyes were distant. "That means war. Open war between witches and vampires."

"Probably," Maggie said, waving a hand vaguely. "But, listen, Delos, the witches sent somebody here, an ambassador, to talk to you. To try to get you on their side. Hunter said they've got one of the Wild Powers on their side already—the witches, I mean. Are you getting this?"

"Of course," Delos said. But now his voice was oddly distant, too. He was looking at something Maggie couldn't see. "But one out of four doesn't matter. Two out of four, three out of four—it's not good enough."

"What are you talking about?" Maggie didn't wait for him

to answer. "But, look. I know the girl who came to talk to you. It's the girl I was with on the rocks, the other one you saved from Bern. She's Aradia, and she's Maiden of all the witches. And, Delos, they're looking for her right now. They want to kill her to stop her from getting to you. And she's my *friend*."

"That's too bad."

"We've got to *stop* them," Maggie said, exasperated.

"We can't."

That brought Maggie up short. She stared at him. "What are you talking about?"

"I'm saying we can't stop them. They're too strong. Maggie, listen to me," he said calmly and clearly, when she began an incoherent protest.

That's the first time he's said my name out loud, she thought dizzily, and then she focused on his words.

"It's not just the spell they've put on me. And it's not just that they control the castle. Oh, yes, they do," he said with a bitter laugh, cutting her off again. "You haven't been here very long; you don't understand. The nobles here are centuries old, most of them. They don't like being ruled by a precocious child with uncanny powers. As soon as Hunter showed up, they transferred their loyalty to him."

"But—"

"He's everything they admire. The perfect vampire, the ultimate predator. He's ruthless and bloodthirsty and he wants to give them the whole world as their hunting grounds. Do you really think any of them can resist that? After years of hunting mindless, bewildered animals that have to be rationed out one at a time? With maybe the odd creaky slave for a special treat? Do you think any of them won't follow him willingly?"

Maggie was silent. There was nothing she could say.

He was right, and it was scary.

"And that isn't all," he continued remorselessly. "Do you want to hear a prophecy?"

"Not really," Maggie said. She'd heard more than enough of those for one lifetime.

He ignored her. "My old teacher used to tell me this," he said.

"Four to stand between the light and the shadow,
Four of blue fire, power in their blood.
Born in the year of the blind Maiden's vision;
Four less one and darkness triumphs."

"Uh-huh," Maggie said. To her it sounded like just more of the same thing. The only interesting thing about it was that it mentioned the blind Maiden. That had to be Aradia, didn't it? She was one famous witch.

"What's 'born in the year of the blind Maiden's vision'?" she asked.

"It means all the Wild Powers are the same age, born seventeen years ago," Delos said impatiently. "But that's not the point.

The point is the last line, 'Four less one and darkness triumphs.' That means that the darkness is going to win, Maggie."

"What do you mean?"

"It's inevitable. There's no way that the humans and the witches can get all four Wild Powers on their side. And if there's even one less than four, the darkness is going to win. All the vampires need to do is kill one of the Wild Powers, and it's all over. Don't you see?"

Maggie stared at him. She did see what he was saying, and it was even scarier than what he'd said before. "But that doesn't mean we can just give up," she said, trying to puzzle out his expression. "If we do that, it *will* be all over. We can't just surrender and *let* them win."

"Of course not," he said harshly. "We have to join them."

There was a long silence. Maggie realized that her mouth had fallen open.

". . . *what?*"

"We have to be on the winning side, and that's the vampire side." He looked at her with yellow eyes that seemed as remote and deathly calm as a panther's. "I'm sorry about your friends, but there's no chance for them. And the only chance for you is to become a vampire."

Maggie's brain suddenly surged into overdrive.

All at once, she saw exactly what he was saying. And fury gave her energy. He was lightning-fast, but she jumped up and out of the way before he could close his hands on her.

"Are you out of your mind?"

"No."

"You're going to *kill* me?"

"I'm going to save your life, the only way I can." He stood up, following her with that same eerie calm.

I can't believe this. I . . . really . . . can't . . . believe this, Maggie thought.

She circled around the bed, then stopped. It was pointless; he was going to get her eventually.

She looked into his face one more time, and saw that he was completely serious. She dropped her arms and relaxed her shoulders, trying to slow her breathing, meeting his eyes directly.

"Delos, this isn't just about me, and it's not just about my friends. It's about all the slaves here, and all the humans on the Outside. Turning me into a vampire isn't going to help them."

"I'm sorry," he said again. "But you're all that really matters."

"No, I'm *not*," Maggie said, and this time the hot tears didn't stop at her eyes, but overflowed and rolled down her cheeks. She shook them off angrily, and took one last deep breath.

"I won't let you," she said.

"You can't stop me."

"I can fight. I can make you kill me before you turn me into a vampire. If you want to try it that way, come and take your best shot."

Delos's yellow eyes bored into hers—and then suddenly shifted and dropped. He stepped back, his face cold.

"Fine," he said. "If you won't cooperate, I'll put you in the dungeon until you see what's best for you."

Maggie felt her mouth drop open again.

"You wouldn't," she said.

"Watch me."

The dungeon, like everything else in the castle, was heart-stoppingly authentic. It had something that Maggie had read about in books but hadn't seen in the rooms above: rushes and straw on the floor. It also had a stone bench carved directly into the stone wall and a narrow, barred window-slit about fifteen feet above Maggie's head. And that was all it had.

Once Maggie had poked into the straw enough to discover that she didn't really *want* to know what was down there and shaken the iron bars that made up the door and examined the stone slabs in the wall and stood on the bench to try to climb to the window, there was nothing else to do. She sat on the bench and felt the true enormity of the situation trickle in on her.

She was really stuck here. Delos was really serious. And the world, the actual, real world out there, could be affected as a consequence.

It wasn't that she didn't understand his motivation. She had been in his mind; she'd felt the strength of his protective-ness for her. And she wanted to protect him, too.

But it wasn't possible to forget about everyone else. Her parents, her friends, her teachers, the paper girl. If she let Delos give up, what happened to them?

Even the people in the Dark Kingdom. Laundress and Old Mender and Soaker and Chamber-pot Emptier and all the other slaves. She *cared* about them. She admired their gritty determination to go on living, whatever the circumstances—and their courage in risking their lives to help her.

That's what Delos doesn't understand, she thought. He doesn't see them as people, so he can't care about them. All his life he's only cared about himself, and now about me. He can't look beyond that.

If only she could think of a way to *make* him see—but she couldn't. As the hours passed and the silence began to wear on her, she kept trying.

No inspiration came. And finally the light outside her cell began to fade and the cold started to settle in.

She was half asleep, huddled on her chilly bench, when she heard the rattle of a key in a door. She jumped up and went to peer through the bars, hoping to see Delos.

The door at the end of the narrow stone corridor opened and someone came in with a flare. But it wasn't Delos. It was a guard, and behind him was another guard, and this one had a prisoner.

"Jeanne!" Maggie said in dismay.

And then her heart plummeted further.

A third guard was half marching, half supporting Aradia.

Maggie looked at them wordlessly.

It wasn't like Jeanne not to fight, she thought, as the guards opened the cell door and shoved the other girls in.

The door clanged shut again, and the guards marched back out without speaking. Almost as an afterthought, one of them stuck a flare in an iron ring to give the prisoners some light.

And then they were gone.

Jeanne picked herself up off the floor, and then helped Aradia get up. "They've got P.J. upstairs," she said to Maggie, who was still staring. "They said they wouldn't hurt her if we went quietly."

Maggie opened her mouth, shut it again, and tried to swallow her heart, which was in her throat. At last she managed to speak.

"Delos said that?"

"Delos and Hunter Redfern and that witch. They're all very chummy."

Maggie sat down on the cold bench.

"I'm sorry," she said.

"Why? Because you're too stupidly trusting?" Jeanne said. "You're not responsible for him."

"I think she means because she's his soulmate," Aradia said softly.

Jeanne stared at her as if she'd started speaking a foreign language. Maggie stared, too, feeling her eyes getting wider, trying to study the beautiful features in the semidarkness.

She felt oddly shy of this girl whom she'd called Cady and who had turned out to be something she could never have imagined.

"How did you know that?" she asked, trying not to sound tongue-tied. "Can you just—tell?"

A smile curved the perfect lips in the shadows. "I could tell before," Aradia said gently, backing up quite accurately to sit on the bench. "When you came back from seeing him the first time, but I was too foggy to really focus on anything then. I've seen a lot of it in the last few years, though. People finding their soulmates, I mean."

"You're better, aren't you?" Maggie said. "You sound lots more—awake." It wasn't just that. Aradia had always had a quiet dignity, but now there was an authority and confidence about her that was new.

"The healing women helped me. I'm still weak, though," Aradia said softly, looking around the cell. "I can't use any of my powers—not that breaking through walls is among them, anyway."

Maggie let her breath out. "Oh, well. I'm glad you're awake, anyway." She added, feeling shy again, "Um, I know your real name now. Sorry about the misunderstanding before."

Aradia put a hand—again perfectly accurately—on Maggie's. "Listen, my dear friend," she said, startling Maggie with both the word and the intensity of her voice, "nobody has ever helped me more than you did, or with less reason. If you'd been one of my people, and you'd known who I was, it would have been amazing enough. But from a human, who didn't know anything about me . . ." She stopped and shook her head. "I don't know if we'll even live through tonight," she said. "But if we do, and if there's ever anything the witches can do for you, all you have to do is ask."

Maggie blinked hard. "Thanks," she whispered. "I mean—you know. I couldn't just leave you."

"I do know," Aradia said. "And that's the amazing thing." She squeezed Maggie's hand. "Whatever happens, I'll never forget you. And neither will the other witches, if I have anything to say about it."

Maggie gulped. She didn't want to get started crying. She was afraid she wouldn't be able to stop.

Fortunately Jeanne was looking back and forth between them like someone at a tennis match. "What's all this sappy stuff?" she demanded. "What are you guys *talking* about?"

Maggie told her. Not just about Aradia being Maiden of the witches, but about everything she'd learned from listening to Hunter Redfern and Sylvia.

"So the witches have left the Night World," Aradia said quietly, when she was finished. "They were about ready to when I left."

"You were coming here to talk to Delos," Maggie said.

Aradia nodded. "We heard that Hunter had gotten some lead about the next Wild Power. And we knew he wasn't going to take any chances on letting Circle Daybreak get hold of this one."

Jeanne was rubbing her forehead. "What's Circle Daybreak?"

"It's the last circle of witches—but it isn't just witches. It's for humans, too, and for shapeshifters and vampires who want to live in peace with humans. And now it's for everybody who opposes the darkness." She thought a moment and added, "I used to belong to Circle Twilight, the . . . not-so-wicked witches." She smiled, then it faded. "But now there are really only two sides to choose from. It's the Daylight or the Darkness, and that's all."

"Delos really isn't on the side of the Darkness," Maggie said, feeling the ache in her chest tighten. "He's just—confused. He'd join you if he didn't think it meant me getting killed."

Aradia squeezed her hand again. "I believe you," she said gently.

"So, you're some kind of bigwig of the witches, huh?" Jeanne said.

Aradia turned toward her and laughed. "I'm their Maiden, the representative of the young witches. If I live long enough, I'll be their Mother one day, and then their Crone."

"What fun. But with all that, you still can't think of any way to get us out of here?"

Aradia sobered. "I can't. I'm sorry. If—this isn't much use, but if I can do anything, it's only to give a prophecy."

Maggie made an involuntary noise in her throat.

"It came while I was asleep in the healer's hut," Aradia said apologetically. "And it was just a thought, a concept. That if there was to be any help in this valley, it was through appealing to people's true hearts."

Jeanne made a much louder and ruder noise than Maggie's.

"There is one more thing," Aradia said, turning her wide unfocused eyes toward Maggie and speaking as gently as ever, "I should have mentioned this earlier. I can tell you about your brother."

CHAPTER 18

Maggie stared at her wildly.

"You . . . what?"

"I *should* have told you earlier," Aradia said. "But I didn't realize he was your brother until my mind became clearer. You're a lot alike, but I couldn't think properly to put it together." She added, quickly and with terrible gentleness, "But, Maggie, I don't want to get your hopes up. I don't think there's much chance he's all right."

Maggie went still. "Tell me."

"He actually saved me before you ever did. I was coming to this valley, but I wasn't alone—there were several other witches with me. We didn't know where the pass was exactly—we'd only managed to get incomplete information from our spies in Hunter Redfern's household."

Maggie controlled her breathing and nodded.

"It was Samhain evening—Halloween. We were wandering

around in the general area of the pass, trying to find a spell that would reveal it. All we did was set off an avalanche."

Maggie stopped breathing entirely. "An avalanche?"

"It didn't hurt your brother. He was on the road, the place we should have been, if we'd only known. But it did kill the others in my party."

"Oh," Maggie whispered. "Oh, I'm sorry . . ."

"I wasn't seriously hurt, but I was completely dazed. I could feel that the others were dead, but I wasn't sure where *I* was anymore. And that was when I heard your brother shouting. He and Sylvia had heard the avalanche, of course, and they came to see if anyone was caught in it."

"Miles would always stop to help people," Maggie said, still almost in a whisper. "Even if they only needed batteries or socks or things."

"I can't tell you how grateful I was to hear him. He saved my life, I'm sure—I would have wandered around dazed until I froze. And I was so happy to recognize that the girl with him was a witch . . ." She grimaced.

"Huh," Jeanne said, but not unsympathetically. "I bet that didn't last."

"She recognized me, too, immediately," Aradia said. "She knew what she had. A hostage to bargain with all the other witches. And to buy credit with Hunter Redfern. And of course, she knew that she could stop me from seeing Delos."

"All she cares about is power," Maggie said quietly. "I heard her talking—it's all about her, and how the witches have given her a bad deal because she's not a Harman or something."

Aradia smiled very faintly. "I'm not a Harman by name, either. But all true witches are daughters of Hellewise Hearth-Woman— if they would just realize it." She shook her head slightly. "Sylvia was so excited about finding me that she couldn't resist explaining it all to your brother. And he . . . wasn't happy."

"No," Maggie said, burning with such fierce pride that for a moment the cold cell seemed warm to her.

"She'd only told him before that she was taking him to some secret place where legends were still alive. But now she told him the truth about the Dark Kingdom, and how she wanted him to be a part of it. She told him that it could be theirs—their own private haven—after Delos left with Hunter Redfern. He could become a vampire or shapeshifter, which- ever he liked better. They would both be part of the Night World, and they could rule here without any interference."

Maggie lifted her hands helplessly, waving them in agita- tion because she couldn't find words. How stupid could Sylvia be? Didn't she know Miles at all?

"Miles wouldn't care about any of that," she finally got out in a choked voice.

"He didn't. He told her so. And I knew right away that he was in trouble with her." Aradia sighed. "But there was nothing I could do. Sylvia played it very cool until they got me down the mountain. She pretended all she cared about was getting me to a doctor and telling the rangers about my friends. But once we were in her apartment, everything changed."

"I remember her apartment," Maggie said slowly. "The people there were weird."

"They were Night People," Aradia said. "And Sylvia's friends. As soon as we were inside she told them what to do. I was trying to explain to Miles, to see if we both could get away, but there were too many of them. He put himself in between me and them, Maggie. He said they'd have to kill him before getting to me."

Maggie's chest felt not so much tight now as swollen, like a drum barrel full of water. She could feel her heart thudding slowly inside, and the way it echoed all through her.

She steadied her voice and said, "Did they kill him?"

"No. Not then. And maybe not ever—but that's the part that I don't know. All I know is that they knocked him out, and then the two slave traders arrived. Bern and Gavin. Sylvia had sent for them."

And they must have come fresh from kidnapping P.J., Maggie thought. What wonderful guys.

"They knocked *me* out. And then Sylvia bound me with spells and practiced with her truth potions on me. She didn't get much information, because I didn't *have* much information. There was no army of witches coming to invade the Dark Kingdom—right now, I wish there were. And she already knew that I was coming to see Delos."

Aradia sighed again and finished quickly. "The truth

potion poisoned me, so that for days afterward I was deliri-
ous. I couldn't really understand what was going on around
me—I just faded in and out. I knew that I was being kept in a
warehouse until the weather cleared enough to take me to the
valley. And I knew that Miles had already been disposed of—
Sylvia mentioned that before she left me in the warehouse. But
I didn't know what she had done with him—and I still don't."

Maggie swallowed. Her heart was still thumping in that
slow, heavy way. "What I don't understand is why she had to
set up a whole scenario to explain where he went. She let some
rangers find her on the mountain, and she said that he fell down
a crevasse. But if he was dead, why not just let him disappear?"

"I think I know the answer to that, at least," Aradia said.
"When Miles was fighting them off he said that his roommates
knew he'd gone climbing with her. He said that if he didn't
come back, they'd remember that."

Yes. It made sense. Everything made sense—except that
Maggie still didn't know what had become of him.

There was a long silence.

"Well, he was brave," Jeanne said finally, and with unexpected seriousness. "If he did die, he went out the right way.
We just ought to hope we can do the same."

Maggie glanced at her, trying to read the angular features
in the darkness. There was no trace of mockery or sarcasm that
she could see.

Well, Cady's changed into Aradia, Maiden of all the

witches, and I've changed into the Deliverer—not that I've been much good at it, she thought. But I think maybe you've changed the most after all, Jeanne—

"You know, I don't even know your last name," she said to Jeanne, so abruptly and so much off the subject that Jeanne reared back a little.

"Uh—McCartney. It was—it *is*—McCartney." She added, "I was fourteen when they got me. I was at the mall playing Fist of Death at the arcade. And I went to go to the bathroom, and it was down this long empty corridor, and the next thing I knew I was waking up in a slave trader's cart. And now you know everything," she said.

Maggie put out a hand in the dimness, "Hi, Jeanne McCartney." She felt the cold grip of slender, callused fingers, and she shook Jeanne's hand. And then she just held on to it, and to Aradia's soft warm fingers on the other side. The three of them sat together in the dark cell, slave, human, and witch Maiden—except that we're really all just girls, Maggie thought.

"You didn't tell me one thing," Maggie said suddenly. "What'd they call you when you started working here? What was your job?"

Jeanne snorted. "Second Assistant Stable Sweeper. And now you know *everything*."

Maggie didn't think she could possibly sleep in a place like this, but after the three of them had sat quietly for a long time she found herself dozing. And when the rattle of the dungeon door startled her, she realized that she'd been asleep.

She had no idea what time it was—the flare was burning low. She could feel Aradia and Jeanne come awake beside her.

"Dinner?" Jeanne muttered.

"I just hope it's not P.J.—" Maggie began, and then broke off as firm, determined steps sounded on the stone floor of the corridor.

She recognized the stride and she stood up to meet Delos.

He stood outside the cell, the dying torchlight flickering on his dark hair, catching occasional sparks off his golden eyes. He was alone.

And he didn't waste time getting to the point.

"I came to see if you've decided to be reasonable," he said.

"I've been reasonable from the beginning," Maggie said quietly and completely seriously. She was searching his face and the slight link she felt between their minds at this distance, hoping to find some change in him. But although she felt turmoil that was almost anguish, she also felt the steel of his resolve.

I won't let you be killed. Nothing else matters.

Maggie felt her shoulders sag.

She turned slightly. Aradia and Jeanne were still sitting on the bench, Aradia motionless, Jeanne coiled and wary. But she could tell that they both felt this was her fight.

And they're right. If I can't do it, nobody can . . . But *how?*

"They're people," she said, gesturing toward the other girls, but watching Delos's face. "I don't know how to get you to see that. They matter, too."

He hardly glanced back at them. "In the time of darkness that is coming," he said, as carefully as if reciting a lesson, "only the Night People will survive. The ancient forces of magic are rising. They've been asleep for ten thousand years, but they're waking up again."

A low voice, not belligerent, but not afraid either, came from the back of the cell. "Some of us believe that humans can learn to live with magic."

"Some of you are idiots and fools and are going to die," Delos said, without even looking.

He stared at Maggie. She stared back at him. They were willing each other as hard as possible to understand.

And I think he's got a stronger will, Maggie thought, as she broke the locked gaze and looked away, thumping the heel of a clenched fist against her forehead.

No. That's not right. I'm Steely Neely and I never give up.

If I tell him that some things are worth dying for . . .

But I don't think *he's* afraid to die. He's just afraid for me. And he just won't listen if I say that *I'd* rather die than see some things happen. But that's the truth. There are some things that you just can't allow to happen, whatever the cost. There are some things that have just got to be stopped.

She froze, and the cell seemed to disappear around her.

She was seeing, in her mind's eye, an equally dark and uncomfortable little cart. And her own voice was saying, *Jeanne. It's got to stop.*

Feeling very light-headed, she turned toward the bench. "Jeanne? Come over here."

Jeanne straightened and walked up doubtfully. She looked into Maggie's face.

Maggie looked at her and then at Delos.

"Now you show him," she said in a voice that was like her own voice, but older and much grimmer, "what his Night People do to slaves who try to escape. Like you showed me."

Jeanne's expression was inscrutable. She went on staring at Maggie for a moment, then she raised her eyebrows and turned around.

She was wearing the same slave tunic she had been wearing for the last four days. She lifted it up in the same way and showed Delos her back.

He took one look and reeled back as if she'd hit him.

Maggie was braced, but even so the backlash of his shock and horror nearly swamped her. She grabbed on to the iron bars of the cell and waited it out, teeth gritted while her vision went from black to red to something like a normal gray.

"*Who did this?*" Delos managed finally, in a voice like ground glass. He was dead white, except for his eyes, which looked black in contrast. "*Who?*"

Jeanne dropped her tunic. "I thought you didn't care about

vermin." And she walked away without answering him, leaving him speechless.

Maggie watched her sit down, then turned back.

"Some things have got to be stopped," she said to Delos. "Do you see what I mean? Some things you just can't let go on."

And then she waited.

I knew he didn't know that kind of thing was happening, she thought, feeling vaguely glad in a very tired, sad, and distant way. But it's good to see it proved.

The silence stretched endlessly.

Delos was still staring at Jeanne. He had run a hand through his hair at some point; it was disheveled and falling over his forehead. The skin of his face seemed to be stretched very tight and his eyes were burning gold.

He looked as if he'd completely lost his bearings, and he didn't know what to trust anymore.

And then he looked at Maggie.

She was still standing there, waiting and watching. Their eyes met and she realized suddenly that she'd never seen him so vulnerable—or so open.

But if there was one thing Prince Delos had, it was resolution. After another moment of helplessness, she saw him straighten his shoulders and draw himself up.

And, as usual, he got directly to the point.

"You're right," he said simply. "And I was wrong. There are some things that have got to be stopped."

Maggie leaned against the bars and smiled.

"I'll get the key," he said, and then went on, briskly planning. "I want the three of you out of the castle, at least, before I confront Hunter."

"You can't do it alone," Maggie began. She should have known he'd immediately start arranging everybody's life again. "Especially not with your power blocked—"

"There's no reason for you to be in any more danger than you have to be," he said. "I'll send you off with some of my people who can be trusted—"

"I'm afraid that won't be possible," a voice said from the corridor.

It gave Maggie a horrible jolt. They were all tired, and all caught up in the moment, and none of them had seen the figure until it was almost behind Delos.

Hunter Redfern was standing there smiling. Sylvia was behind him. And behind *them*, crowded together, were armed guards.

"We've had to dispose of the few idiots who insisted on remaining loyal to you," Hunter said amiably. His eyes were shining like the purest gold. "The castle is now under our control. But do go on with your plans, it's very sweet to hear you trying to save each other."

"And it's no use trying to pretend," Sylvia added spitefully. "We heard everything. We knew you couldn't be trusted, so we let you come down here on purpose, to see what you'd say."

For someone who'd known Delos a while, she didn't understand him very well, Maggie thought. Maggie could have told her that pretending was the last thing that would occur to Delos. Instead he did what Maggie knew he would; he launched himself at Hunter Redfern's throat.

Delos was young and strong and very angry—but it was no contest. After Sylvia had squeaked and withdrawn, the guards all came to help Hunter. After that it was over quickly.

"Put him in with his friends," Hunter said, brushing off his sleeves. "It's a real pity to see my only surviving heir come to this," he added, once Delos had been kicked and thrown into the cell. For a moment there was that note of genuine feeling in his voice that Maggie had heard before. Then the golden eyes went cold and more bitter than ever. "I think tomorrow morning we'll have a very special hunt," he said. "And then there will be only three Wild Powers to worry about."

This time, when the guards left, they took all the flares with them.

"I'm sorry," Maggie whispered, trying to inspect Delos's bruises by touch alone. "Delos, I'm sorry . . . I didn't know . . ."

"It doesn't matter," he said, holding her hands. "It would have happened eventually anyway."

"For a vampire, you didn't put up much of a fight," Jeanne's voice came from the back of the cell.

Maggie frowned, but Delos turned toward her and spoke without defensiveness. "That witch bound more than just the blue fire when she put this spell on my arm," he said. "She took all my vampire powers. I'm essentially a human until she removes it."

"Aradia?" Maggie said. "Can you do anything? I mean, I know only Sylvia is supposed to be able to take the spell off, but . . ."

Aradia knelt beside them, graceful in the darkness. She touched Delos's arm gently, then sighed.

"I'm sorry," she said. "Even if I were at full power, there's nothing I could do."

Maggie let out her breath.

"That's the only thing I regret," Delos said. "That I can't save you."

"You have to stop thinking about that," Maggie whispered.

She was filled with a strange resignation. It wasn't that she was giving up. But she was very tired, physically and emotionally, and there was nothing she could do right now. . . .

And maybe nothing ever, she thought dimly. She felt something steadying her and realized it was Delos's arm. She leaned against him, glad of his warmth and solidity in the darkness. There was a tremendous comfort in just being held by him.

Sometimes just having fought is important, she thought. Even if you don't win.

Her eyelids were terribly heavy. It felt absolutely wonderful to close them, just for a moment . . .

She only woke up once during the night, and that was

because of Delos. She could sense something in him—something in his mind. He seemed to be asleep, but very far away, and very agitated.

Was he calling my name? she wondered. I thought I heard that . . .

He was thrashing and muttering, now. Maggie leaned close and caught a few words.

"I love you . . . I did love you . . . always remember that . . ."

"Delos!" She shook him. "Delos, what are you doing?"

He came awake with a start.

"Nothing."

But she knew. She remembered those words—she'd heard them before she had actually met Delos on the mountain.

"It was my dream. You were . . . going back in time somehow, weren't you? And giving me that dream I had, warning me to get away from this valley." She frowned. "But how can you? I thought you couldn't use your powers."

"I don't think this took vampire powers," he said, sounding almost guilty. "It was more—I think it was just the bond between us. The soulmate thing. I don't even know how I did it. I just—went to sleep and started dreaming about the you of the past. It was as if I was searching for you—and then I found you. I made the connection. I don't know if it's ever been done before, that kind of time travel."

Maggie shook her head. "But you already know it didn't work. The dream didn't change anything. I didn't leave as soon as I woke up in the cart, because I'm here. And if I *had* left, I would never have met you, and then you wouldn't have sent the dream. . . ."

"I know," he said, and his voice was tired and a bit forlorn. He sounded very young, just then. "But it was worth a try."

CHAPTER 19

The hunt of your lives," Hunter Redfern said. He was standing handsome and erect, smiling easily. The nobles were gathered around him, and Maggie even saw some familiar faces in the crowd.

That rough man from Delos's memories—the one who grabbed his arm, she thought dreamily. And the woman who put the first binding spell on him.

They were crowded in the courtyard, their faces eager. The first pale light was just touching the sky—not that the sun was visible, of course. But it was enough to turn the clouds pearly and cast an eerie, almost greenish luminescence over the scene below.

"Two humans, a witch, and a renegade prince," Hunter proclaimed. He was enjoying himself hugely, Maggie could tell. "You'll never have another chance at prey like this."

Maggie gripped Delos's hand tightly.

She was frightened but at the same time strangely proud. If the nobles around Hunter were expecting their prey to cower or beg, they were going to be disappointed.

They were alone, the four of them, in a little empty space in the square. Maggie and Aradia and Jeanne in their slave clothes, Delos in his leggings and shirtsleeves. A little wind blew and stirred Maggie's hair, but otherwise they were perfectly still.

Aradia, of course, was always dignified. Just now her face was grave and sad, but there was no sign of anger or fear in it. She stood at her full height, her huge clear eyes turned toward the crowd, as if they were all welcome guests that she had invited.

Jeanne was more rumpled. Her red hair was disheveled and her tunic was wrinkled, but there was a grim smile on her angular face and a wild battle light in her green eyes. She was one prey that was going to fight, Maggie knew.

Maggie herself was doing her best to live up to the others. She stood as tall as she could, knowing she would never be as impressive as Aradia, or as devil-may-care as Jeanne, but trying at least to look as if dying came easy to her.

Delos was magnificent.

In his shirtsleeves, he was more of a prince than Hunter Redfern would ever be. He looked at the crowd of nobles who had all promised to be loyal to him and were now thirsting for his blood—and he didn't get mad.

He tried to talk to them.

"Watch what happens here," he said, his voice carrying easily across the square. "And don't forget it. Are you really going to follow a man who can do this to his own great-grandson? How long is it going to be before he turns on *you*? Before you find yourselves in front of a pack of hunting animals?"

"Shut him up," Hunter said. He tried to say it jovially, but Maggie could hear the fury underneath.

And the command didn't seem to make much sense. Maggie could see the nobles looking at each other—who was supposed to shut him up, and how?

"There are some things that have to be stopped," Delos said. "And this man is one of them. I admit it, I was willing to go along with him—but that was because I was blind and stupid. I know better now—and I knew better before he turned against me. You all know me. Would I be standing here, willing to give up my life for no reason?"

There was the tiniest stirring among the nobles.

Maggie looked at them hopefully—and then her heart sank.

They simply weren't used to thinking for themselves, or maybe they were used to thinking only *of* themselves. But she could tell there wasn't material for a rebellion here.

And the slaves weren't going to be of any help, either. The guards had weapons, they didn't. They were frightened, they were unhappy, but this kind of hunt was something they'd seen before. They knew that it couldn't be stopped.

"This girl came to us peacefully, trying to keep the alliance between witches and vampire," Delos was saying, his hand on Aradia's shoulder. "And in return we tried to kill her. I'm telling you right now, that by spilling her innocent blood, you're all committing a crime that will come back to haunt you."

Another little stirring—among women, Maggie thought. Witches, maybe?

"Shut him *up*," Hunter said, almost bellowing it.

And this time he seemed to be saying it to a specific person. Maggie followed his gaze and saw Sylvia near them.

"Some beasts have to be muzzled before they can be hunted," Hunter said, looking straight at Sylvia. "So take care of it now. The hunt is about to begin."

Sylvia stepped closer to Delos, a little uneasily. He stared back at her levelly, as if daring her to wonder what he'd do when she got nearer.

"Guards!" Hunter Redfern said, sounding tired.

The guards moved in. They had two different kinds of lances, a distant part of Maggie's mind noted. One tipped with metal—that must be for humans and witches—and one tipped with wood.

For vampires, she thought. If Delos wasn't careful, he might get skewered in the heart before the hunt even began.

"Now shut his lying mouth," Hunter Redfern said.

Sylvia took her basket off her arm.

"In the new order after the millennium, we'll have hunts

like this every day," Hunter Redfern was saying, trying to undo the damage that his great-grandson had done. "Each of us will have a city of humans to hunt. A city of throats to cut, a city of flesh to eat."

Sylvia was fishing in her basket, not afraid to stand close to the vampire prince since he was surrounded by a forest of lances.

"Sylvia," Aradia said quietly.

Sylvia looked up, startled. Maggie saw her eyes, the color of violets.

"Each of us will be a prince—" Hunter Redfern was saying.

"Sylvia Weald," Aradia said.

Sylvia looked down. "Don't talk to me," she whispered. "You're not—I'm not one of you anymore."

"All you have to do is follow me," Hunter was saying.

"Sylvia Weald," Aradia said. "You were born a witch. Your name means the greenwood, the sacred grove. You are a daughter of Hellewise, and you will be until you die. You are my sister."

"I am not," Sylvia spat.

"You can't help it. Nothing can break the bond. In your deepest heart you know that. And as Maiden of all the witches, and in the name of Hellewise Hearth-Woman, I adjure you: *remove your spell from this boy.*"

It was the strangest thing—but it didn't seem to be Aradia who said it. Oh, it was Aradia's voice, all right, Maggie thought, and it was Aradia standing there. But at that moment she seemed to be fused with another form—a sort of shining aura all around her. Someone who was part of her, but more than she was.

It looked, Maggie thought dizzily, like a tall woman with hair as pale as Sylvia's and large brown eyes.

Sylvia gasped out, "Hellewise . . ." Her own violet eyes were huge and frightened.

Then she just stood frozen.

Hunter was ranting on. Maggie could hear him vaguely, but all she could see was Sylvia, the shudders that ran through Sylvia's frame, the heaving of Sylvia's chest.

Appeal to their true hearts, Maggie thought.

"Sylvia," she said. "I believe in you."

The violet eyes turned toward her, amazed.

"I don't care what you did to Miles," Maggie said. "I know you're confused—I know you were unhappy. But now you have a chance to make up for it. You can do something—something *important* here. Something that will change the world."

"Rivers of blood," Hunter was raving. "And no one to stop us. We won't stop with enslaving the humans. The witches are our enemies now. Think of the power you'll feel when you drink their lives!"

"If you let this Wild Power be killed, *you'll* be responsible for the darkness coming," Maggie said. "Only you. Because you're the only one who can stop it *right now.*"

Sylvia put a trembling hand to her cheek. She looked as if she were about to faint

"Do you really want to go down in history as the one who destroyed the world?" Maggie said.

"As Maiden of all the witches . . . ," Aradia said.

And another, deeper voice seemed to follow on hers like an echo, *As Mother of all the witches . . .*

"And in the name of Hellewise . . ."

And in the name of my children . . .

"As you are a Hearth-Woman . . ."

As you are my own daughter, a true Hearth-Woman . . .

"*I adjure you!*" Aradia said, and her voice rang out in double tones so clearly that it actually stopped Hunter in mid-tirade.

It stopped everyone. For an instant there was absolutely no sound in the courtyard. Everyone was looking around to see where the voice had come from.

Sylvia was simply staring at Aradia.

Then the violet eyes shut and her entire body shivered in a sigh.

When she spoke it was on the barest whisper of breath, and only someone as close as Maggie was could have heard her.

"As a daughter of Hellewise, I obey."

And then she was reaching for Delos's arm, and Delos was reaching toward her. And Hunter was shouting wildly, but Maggie couldn't make out the words. She couldn't make out

Sylvia's words, either, but she saw her lips move, and she saw the slender pale fingers clasp Delos's wrist.

And saw the lance coming just before it pierced Sylvia's heart.

Then, as if everything came into focus at once, she realized what Hunter had been shouting in a voice so distorted it was barely recognizable.

"Kill her! Kill her!"

And that's just what they'd done, Maggie thought, her mind oddly clear, even as a wave of horror and pity seemed to engulf her body. The lance went right through Sylvia. It knocked her backward, away from Delos, and blood spurted all over the front of Sylvia's beautiful green dress.

And Sylvia looked toward Hunter Redfern and smiled. This time Maggie could read the words on her lips.

"Too late."

Delos turned. There was red blood on his white shirt—his own, Maggie realized. He'd tried to get in the way of the guard's killing Sylvia. But now he had eyes only for his great-grandfather.

"It stops *here*!"

She had seen the blue fire before, but never like this. The blast was like a nuclear explosion. It struck where Hunter Redfern was standing with his most loyal nobles around him, and then it shot up into the sky in a pillar of electric blue. And it went on and on, from sky to earth and back again, as if the sun were falling in front of the castle.

CHAPTER 20

Maggie held Sylvia gently. Or at least, she knelt by her and tried to hold her as best she could without disturbing the piece of broken spear that was still lodged in Sylvia's body.

It was all over. Where Hunter Redfern and his most trusted nobles had been, there was a large scorched crater in the earth. Maggie vaguely recalled seeing a few people running for the hills—Gavin the slave trader had been among them. But Hunter hadn't been one of them. He had been at ground zero when the blue fire struck, and now there wasn't even a wisp of red hair to show that he had existed.

Except for Delos, there weren't any Night People left in the courtyard at all.

The slaves were just barely peeking out again from their huts.

"It's all right," Jeanne was yelling. "Yeah, you heard me—*it's all right!* Delos isn't dangerous. Not to us, anyway. Come on, you, get out of there—what are you doing hiding behind that pig?"

"She's good at this," a grim voice murmured.

Maggie looked up and saw a tall, gaunt figure, with a very small girl clasped to her side.

"Laundress!" she said. "Oh, and P.J.—I'm so glad you're all right. But, Laundress, please . . ."

The healing woman knelt. But even as she did, a look passed between her and Sylvia. Sylvia's face was a strange, chalky color, with shadows that looked like bruises under her eyes. There was a little blood at the corner of her mouth.

"It's no good," she said thickly.

"She's right," Laundress said bluntly. "There's nothing you can do to help this one, Deliverer, and nothing I can do, either."

"I'm not anybody's Deliverer," Maggie said. Tears prickled behind her eyes.

"You could have fooled me," Laundress said, and got up again. "I see you sitting here, and I see all the slaves over there, free. You came and it happened—the prophecies were fulfilled. If you didn't do it, it's a strange coincidence."

The look in her dark eyes, although as unsentimental as ever, made Maggie's cheeks burn suddenly. She looked back down at Sylvia.

"But she's the one who saved us," she said, hardly aware

that she was speaking out loud. "She deserves some kind of dignity. . . ."

"She's not the only one who saved us," a voice said quietly, and Maggie looked up gratefully at Delos.

"No, you did, too."

"That's not what I meant," he said, and knelt where Laundress had. One of his hands touched Maggie's shoulder lightly, but the other one went to Sylvia's.

"There's only one thing I can do to help you," he said. "Do you want it?"

"To become a vampire?" Sylvia's head moved slightly in a negative. "No. And since there's wood next to my heart right now, I don't think it would work anyway."

Maggie gulped and looked at the spear, which had cracked in the confusion when the guards ran. "We could take it out—"

"I wouldn't live through it. Give up for once, will you?" Sylvia's head moved slightly again in disgust. Maggie had to admire her; even dying, she still had the strength to be nasty. Witches were tough.

"Listen," Sylvia said, staring at her. "There's something I want to tell you." She drew a painful breath. "About your brother."

Maggie swallowed, braced to hear the terrible details. "Yes."

"It really bugged me, you know? I would put on my nicest clothes, do my hair, we would go out . . . and then he'd talk about *you*."

Maggie blinked, utterly nonplussed. This wasn't at all what she had expected. "He would?"

"About *his sister.* How brave she was. How smart she was. How stubborn she was."

Maggie kept blinking. She'd heard Miles accuse her of lots of things, but never of being smart. She felt her eyelids prickle again and her throat swell painfully.

"He couldn't stand to hear a bad word about you," Sylvia was saying. Her purple-shadowed eyes narrowed suddenly, the color of bittersweet nightshade. "And I hated you for that. But him . . . I liked him."

Her voice was getting much weaker. Aradia knelt on her other side and touched the shimmering silvery hair.

"You don't have long," she said quietly, as if giving a warning.

Sylvia's eyes blinked once, as if to say she understood. Then she turned her eyes on Maggie.

"I told Delos I killed him," she whispered. "But . . . I lied."

Maggie felt her eyes fly open. Then all at once her heart was beating so hard that it shook her entire body.

"You *didn't* kill him? He's alive?"

"I wanted to punish him . . . but I wanted him near me, too. . . ."

A wave of dizziness broke over Maggie. She bent over Sylvia, trying not to clutch at the slender shoulders. All she could see was Sylvia's pale face.

"Please tell me what you did," she whispered with passionate intensity. "Please tell me."

"I had him . . . changed." The musical voice was only a distant murmur now. "Made him a shapeshifter . . . and added a spell. So he wouldn't be human again until I wanted . . ."

"What kind of spell?" Aradia prompted quietly.

Sylvia made a sound like the most faraway of sighs. "Not anything that *you* need to deal with, Maiden. . . . Just take the leather band off his leg. He'll always be a shapeshifter . . . but he won't be lost to you. . . ."

Suddenly her voice swelled up a little stronger, and Maggie realized that the bruised eyes were looking at her with something like Sylvia's old malice.

"You're so smart . . . I'm sure you can figure out which animal . . ."

After that a strange sound came out of her throat, one that Maggie had never heard before. Somehow she knew without being told that it meant Sylvia was dying—right then.

The body in the green dress arched up once and went still. Sylvia's head fell back. Her eyes, the color of tear-drenched violets, were open, staring up at the sky, but they seemed oddly flat.

Aradia put a slender dark hand on the pale forehead.

"Goddess of Life, receive this daughter of Hellewise," she said in her soft, ageless voice. "Guide her to the other world." She added, in a whisper, "She takes with her the blessing of all the witches."

Maggie looked up almost fearfully to see if the shining figure who had surrounded Aradia like an aura would come back. But all she saw was Aradia's beautiful face, with its smooth skin the color of coffee with cream and its compassionate blind gaze.

Then Aradia gently moved her hand down to shut Sylvia's eyes.

Maggie clenched her teeth, but it was no use. She gasped once, and then somehow she was in the middle of sobbing violently, unable to stop it. But Delos's arms were around her, and she buried her face in his neck, and that helped. When she got control of herself a few minutes later, she realized that in his arms she felt almost what she had in her dream, that inexpressible sense of peace and security. Of belonging, utterly.

As long as her soulmate was alive, and they were together, she would be all right.

Then she noticed that P.J. was pressed up against her, too, and she let go of Delos to put one arm around the small shaking body.

"You okay, kiddo?" she whispered.

P.J. sniffed. "Yeah. I am now. It's been pretty scary, but I'm glad it's over."

"And you know," Jeanne said, looking down at Sylvia with her hands on her hips, "that's how I want to go. Taking my own way out . . . and totally pissing everybody off at the end."

Maggie glanced up, startled, and choked. Then she gurgled.

Then she shook her head, and knew that her crying spell was over. "I don't even know why I'm like this about her. She wasn't a nice person. I wanted to kill her myself."

"She was a person," Delos said.

Which, Maggie decided, was about the best summing-up anybody could provide.

She realized that Jeanne and Laundress and Delos were looking at her intently, and that Aradia's face was turned her way.

"Well?" Jeanne said. "*Do* you know? Which animal your brother is?"

"Oh," Maggie said. "I think so."

She looked at Delos. "Do you happen to know what the name Gavin means? For a shapeshifter? Does it mean falcon?"

His black-lashed golden eyes met hers. "Hawk or falcon. Yes."

Warm pleasure filled Maggie.

"Then I know," she said simply. She stood up, and Delos came with her as if he belonged by her. "How can we find the falcon she had with her that first day we met? When you were out with the hunting party?"

"It should be in the mews," Delos said.

A fascinated crowd gathered behind them as they went. Maggie recognized Old Mender, smiling and cackling, and Soaker, not looking frightened anymore, and Chamber-pot Emptier . . .

"We really need to get you guys some new names," she muttered. "Can you just pick one or something?"

The big girl with the moon face and the gentle eyes smiled at her shyly. "I heard of a noble named Hortense once. . . ."

"That's good," Maggie said, after just the slightest pause. "Yeah, that's great. I mean, comparatively."

They reached the mews, which was a dark little room near the stable, with perches all over the walls. The falcons were upset and distracted, and the air was full of flapping wings. They all looked alike to Maggie.

"It would be a new bird," Delos said. "I think maybe that one. Is the falconer here?"

While everyone milled around looking for him, Jeanne edged close to Maggie.

"What I want to know is how you know. How did you even know Gavin was a shapeshifter at all?"

"I didn't—but it was sort of logical. After all, Bern was one. They both seemed to have the same kind of senses. And Aradia said that Sylvia took care of Miles down at her apartment, and Bern and Gavin were both there. So it seemed natural that maybe she made one of them pass the curse along to Miles."

"But why did you figure Gavin was a *falcon*?"

"I don't know," Maggie said slowly, "I just—well, he looked a little bit like one. Sort of thin and golden. But it was more things that happened—he got away from Delos and over to the hunting party too fast to have gone by ground. I didn't really think about it much then, but it must have stuck at the back of my mind."

Jeanne gave her a narrow sideways glance. "Still doesn't sound like enough."

"No—but mostly, it was that *Miles* just had to be a falcon. It had to be something small—Sylvia would hardly be carrying a pig or a tiger or a bear around with her up the mountain. And I saw her with a falcon that first day. It was something she *could* keep near her, something that she could control. Something that was an—accessory. It just all made sense."

Jeanne made a sound like *hmph*. "I still don't think you're a rocket scientist. I think you lucked out."

Maggie turned as the crowd brought a little man with a lean, shrewd face to her—Falconer. "Well, we don't know yet," she murmured fervently. "But I sure hope so."

The little man held up a bird. "This is the new one. Lady Sylvia said never to take the green band off his leg—but I've got a knife. Would you like to do it?"

Maggie held her breath. She tried to keep her hand steady as she carefully cut through the emerald green leather band, but her fingers trembled.

The leather tie fell free—and for a moment her heart stood still, because nothing happened.

And then she saw it. The rippling change as the bird's wings outstretched and thickened and the feathers merged and swam . . . and then Falconer was moving back, and a human form was taking shape. . . .

And then Miles was standing there, with his auburn hair shining red gold and his handsome, wicked smile.

He gave her the thumbs-up sign.

"Hey, I knew you would rescue me. What are little sisters for?" he said—and then Maggie was in his arms.

It seemed a long time later that all the hugging and crying and explaining was done. The slaves—the *ex*-slaves, Maggie corrected herself—had begun to gather and organize themselves and make plans. Delos and Aradia had sent various messengers out of the valley.

There were still things to be settled—months' and years' worth of things. And Maggie knew that life would never be the same for her again. She would never be a normal schoolgirl.

Her brother was a shapeshifter—well, at least it was a form he could enjoy, she thought wryly. He was already talking to Jeanne about a new way of getting to the summits of mountains—with wings.

Her soulmate was a Wild Power. Aradia had already told her what that meant. It meant that they would have to be protected by the witches and Circle Daybreak until the time of darkness came and Delos was needed, so that the Night World didn't kill them. And even if they survived until the final battle . . . it was going to be a tough one.

Plus, she herself had changed forever. She felt she owed something to the people of the valley, who were still calling her the Deliverer. She would have to try to help them adjust to the Outside world. Her fate would be intertwined with theirs all her life.

But just now, everybody was talking about getting some food.

"Come into the castle—all of you," Delos said simply.

He took Maggie's arm and started toward it. Just then P.J. pointed to the sky, and there was an awed murmur from the crowd.

"The sun!"

It was true. Maggie looked up and was dazzled. In the smooth, pearly sky of the Dark Kingdom, in exactly the place where the blue fire had flashed from the earth, there was a little clearing in the clouds. The sun was shining through, chasing away the mist, turning the trees in the surrounding hills emerald green.

And glinting off the sleek black walls of the castle like a mirror.

A place of enchantment, Maggie thought, looking around in wonder. It really is beautiful here.

Then she looked at the boy beside her. At his dark hair—just now extremely tousled—and his smooth fair skin, and his elegant bones. At the mouth, which was still a bit proud and willful, but was mostly vulnerable.

And at those fearless, brilliant yellow eyes, which looked back at her as if she were the most important thing in the universe.

"I suppose that all prophecies come true by accident," she said slowly and thoughtfully. "From just ordinary people trying and lucking out."

"There is *nothing* ordinary about you," Delos said, and kissed her.

One from the land of kings long forgotten;
One from the hearth which still holds the spark;
One from the Day World where two eyes are watching;
One from the twilight to be one with the dark.

The Night World
lives on in *Witchlight,*
by L. J. Smith.

T he mall was so peaceful. There was no hint of the terrible thing that was about to happen.

It looked like any other shopping mall in North Carolina on a Sunday afternoon in December. Modern. Brightly decorated. Crowded with customers who knew there were only ten shopping days until Christmas. Warm, despite the chilly gray skies outside. Safe.

Not the kind of place where a monster would appear.

Keller walked past a display of "Santa Claus Through the Ages" with all her senses alert and open. And that meant a lot of senses. The glimpses she caught of herself in darkened store windows showed a high-school-aged girl in a sleek jumpsuit, with straight black hair that fell past her hips and cool gray eyes. But she knew that anybody who watched her closely was likely to see something else—a sort of prowling grace in the way she walked and an inner glow when the gray eyes focused on anything.

Raksha Keller didn't look quite human. Which was hardly surprising, because she wasn't. She was a shapeshifter, and if people looking at her got the impression of a half-tamed panther on the loose, they were getting it exactly right.

"Okay, everybody." Keller touched the pin on her collar, then pressed a finger to the nearly invisible receiver in her ear, trying to tune out the Christmas music that filled the mall. "Report in."

"Winnie here." The voice that spoke through the receiver was light, almost lilting, but professional. "I'm over by Sears. Haven't seen anything yet. Maybe she's not here."

"Maybe," Keller said shortly into the pin—which wasn't a pin at all but an extremely expensive transmission device. "But she's supposed to love shopping, and her parents said she was headed this way. It's the best lead we've got. Keep looking."

"Nissa here." This voice was cooler and softer, emotionless. "I'm in the parking lot, driving by the Bingham Street entrance. Nothing to report—wait." A pause, then the ghostly voice came back with a new tension: "Keller, we've got trouble. A black limo just pulled up outside Brody's. They know she's here."

Keller's stomach tightened, but she kept her voice level. "You're sure it's them?"

"I'm sure. They're getting out—a couple of vampires and . . . something else. A young guy, just a boy really. Maybe a shapeshifter. I don't know for sure; he isn't like anything I've seen before." The voice was troubled, and that troubled Keller. Nissa Johnson was a vampire with a brain like the Library of Congress. Something *she* didn't recognize?

"Should I park and come help you?" Nissa asked.

"No," Keller said sharply. "Stay with the car; we're going to need it for a fast getaway. Winnie and I will take care of it. Right, Winnie?"

"Oh, right, Boss. In fact, I can take 'em all on myself; you just watch."

"*You* watch your mouth, girl." But Keller had to fight the grim smile that was tugging at her lips. Winfrith Arlin was Nissa's opposite—a witch and inclined to be emotional. Her odd sense of humor had lightened some black moments.

"Both of you stay alert," Keller said, completely serious now. "You know what's at stake."

"Right, Boss." This time, both voices were subdued.

They did know.

The world.

The girl they were looking for could save the world—or destroy it. Not that she knew that . . . yet. Her name was Iliana Harman, and she had grown up as a human child. She didn't realize that she had the blood of witches in her and that she was one of the four Wild Powers destined to fight against the time of darkness that was coming.

She's about to get quite a surprise when we tell her, Keller thought.

That was assuming that Keller's team got to her before the bad guys did. But they would. They had to. There was a reason they'd been chosen to come here, when every agent of Circle Daybreak in North America would have been glad to do this job.

They were the best. It was that simple.

They were an odd team—vampire, witch, and shape-shifter—but they were unbeatable. And Keller was only seventeen, but she already had a reputation for never losing.

And I'm not about to blow that now, she thought, "This is it, kiddies," she said. "No more talking until we ID the girl. Good luck." Their transmissions were scrambled, of course, but there was no point in taking chances. The bad guys were extremely well organized.

Doesn't matter. We'll still win, Keller thought, and she paused in her walking long enough *really* to expand her senses.

It was like stepping into a different world. They were senses that a human couldn't even imagine. Infrared. She saw body heat. Smell. Humans didn't have any sense of smell, not really. Keller could distinguish Coke from Pepsi from across a room. Touch. As a panther, Keller had exquisitely sensitive hairs all over her body, especially on her face. Even in human form, she could feel things with ten times the intensity of a real human. She could feel her way in total darkness by the air pressure on her skin.

Hearing. She could hear both higher and lower pitches

than a human, and she could pinpoint an individual cough in a crowd. Sight. She had night vision like—well, like a cat's.

Not to mention more than five hundred muscles that she could move voluntarily.

And just now, all her resources were attuned to finding one teenage girl in this swarming mall. Her eyes roved over faces; her ears pricked at the sound of every young voice; her nose sorted through thousands of smells for the one that would match the T-shirt she'd taken from Iliana's room.

Then, just as she froze, catching a whiff of something familiar, the receiver in her ear came to life.

"Keller—I spotted her! Hallmark, second floor. But they're here, too."

They'd found her first.

Keller cursed soundlessly. Aloud, she said, "Nissa, bring the car around to the west side of the mall. Winnie, don't do anything. I'm coming."

The nearest escalator was at the end of the mall. But from the map in her hand, she could see that Hallmark was directly above her on the upper level. And she couldn't waste time.

Keller gathered her legs under her and jumped.

One leap, straight up. She ignored the gasps—and a few shrieks—of the people around her as she sprang. At the top of her jump, she caught the railing that fenced off the upper-level walkway. She hung for a second by her hands, then pulled herself up smoothly.

More people were staring. Keller ignored them. They got out of her way as she headed for the Hallmark store.

Winnie was standing with her back to the display window of the store beside it. She was short, with a froth of strawberry curls and a pixie face. Keller edged up to her, careful to keep out of the line of sight of the Hallmark.

"What's up?"

"There's three of them," Winnie murmured in a barely audible voice. "Just like Nissa said. I saw them go in—and then I saw her. They've got her surrounded, but so far they're just talking to her." She glanced sideways at Keller with dancing green eyes. "Only three—we can take them easy."

"Yeah, and that's what worries me. Why would they only send three?"

Winnie shrugged slightly. "Maybe they're like us—the best."

Keller only acknowledged that with a flicker of her eyebrows. She was edging forward centimeter by centimeter, trying to get a glimpse of the interior of the Hallmark shop between the stockings and stuffed animals in the display window.

There. Two guys in dark clothing almost like uniforms—vampire thugs. Another guy Keller could see only as a partial silhouette through a rack of Christmas ornaments.

And her. Iliana. The girl everybody wanted.

She was beautiful, almost impossibly so. Keller had seen a picture, and it had been beautiful, but now she saw that it hadn't come within miles of conveying the real girl. She had the silvery-fair hair and violet eyes that showed her Harman blood. She also had an extraordinary delicacy of features and grace of movement that made her as pretty to watch as a white kitten on the grass. Although Keller knew she was seventeen, she seemed slight and childlike. Almost fairylike. And right now, she was listening with wide, trusting eyes to whatever the silhouette guy was saying.

To Keller's fury, she couldn't make it out. He must be whispering.

"It's really her," Winnie breathed from beside Keller, awed. "The Witch Child. She looks just like the legends said, just like I imagined." Her voice turned indignant. "I can't stand to watch *them* talk to her. It's like—blasphemy."

"Keep your hair on," Keller murmured, still searching with her eyes. "You witches get so emotional about your legends."

"Well, we should. She's not just a Wild Power, she's a pure soul." Winfrith's voice was softly awed. "She must be so wise, so gentle, so farsighted. I can't wait to talk to her." Her voice sharpened. "And those thugs shouldn't be *allowed* to talk to her. Come on, Keller, we can take them fast. Let's go."

"Winnie, don't—"

It was too late. Winnie was already moving, heading straight into the shop without any attempt at concealment.

Keller cursed again. But she didn't have any choice now. "Nissa, stand by. Things are going to get exciting," she snapped, touching her pin, and then she followed.

Winnie was walking directly toward the little group of three guys and Iliana as Keller reached the door. The guys were looking up, instantly alert. Keller saw their faces and gathered herself for a leap.

But it never happened. Before she could get all her muscles ready, the silhouette guy turned—and everything changed.

Time went into slow motion. Keller saw his face clearly, as if she'd had a year to study it. He wasn't bad-looking—quite handsome, actually. He didn't look much older than she was, and he had clean, nicely molded features. He had a small, compact body with what looked like hard muscles under his clothes. His hair was black, shaggy but shiny, almost like fur. It fell over his forehead in an odd way, a way that looked deliberately disarrayed and was at odds with the neatness of the rest of him.

And he had eyes of obsidian.

Totally opaque.

Shiny silver-black, with nothing clear or transparent about them. They revealed nothing; they simply threw light back at anyone who looked into them. They were the eyes of a monster, and every one of Keller's five hundred voluntary muscles froze in fear.

She didn't need to hear the roar that was far below the pitch that human ears could pick up. She didn't need to see the swirl of dark energy that flared like a red-tinged black aura around him. She knew already, instinctively, and she tried to get the breath to yell a warning to Winnie.

There was no time.

She could only watch as the boy's face turned toward Winnie and power exploded out of him.

He did it so casually. Keller could tell that it was only a flick of his mind, like a horse slapping its tail at a fly. But the dark power slammed into Winnie and sent her flying through the air, arms and legs outstretched, until she hit a wall covered with display plates and clocks. The crash was tremendous.

Winnie! Keller almost yelled it out loud.

Winnie fell behind the cash register counter, out of Keller's line of sight. Keller couldn't tell if she were alive or not. The cashier who had been standing behind the counter went running and screaming toward the back of the shop. The customers scattered, some following the cashier, some dashing for the exit.

Keller hung in the doorway a second longer as they streamed out around her. Then she reeled away to stand with her back against the window of the next shop, breathing hard. There were coils of ice in her guts.

A dragon.

He was a *dragon.*

They'd gotten a dragon.

Keller's heart was pounding.

Somehow, somewhere, the people of the Night World had found one and awakened him. And they'd paid him—bribed him—to join their side. Keller didn't even want to imagine what the price might have been. Bile rose in her throat, and she swallowed hard.

Dragons were the oldest and most powerful of the shape-shifters, and the most evil. They had all gone to sleep thirty thousand years ago—or, rather, they had been put to sleep by the witches. Keller didn't know exactly how it had been done, but all the old legends said the world had been better off since.

And now one was back.

But he might not be fully awake yet. From the glimpse she'd had, his body was still cold, not much heat radiating from it. He'd be sluggish, not mentally alert.

It was the chance of a lifetime.

Keller's decision was made in that instant. There was no time to think about it—and no need. The inhabitants of the Night World wanted to destroy the human world. And there were plenty of them to do it, vampires and dark witches and ghouls. But *this* was something in another league altogether. With a dragon on their side, the Night World would easily crush Circle Daybreak and all other forces that wanted to save the humans from the end of the world that was coming. It would be no contest.

And as for that little girl in there, Iliana the Witch Child, the Wild Power meant to help save humankind—she would get swatted like a bug if she didn't obey the dragon.

Keller couldn't let that happen.

Even as Keller was thinking it, she was changing. It was strange to do it in a public place, in front of people. It went against all her most deeply ingrained training. But she didn't have time to dwell on that.

It felt good. It always did. Painful in a nice way, like the feeling of having a tight bandage removed. A release.

Her body was changing. For a moment, she didn't feel like anything—she almost had no body. She was fluid, a being of pure energy, with no more fixed form than a candle flame. She was utterly . . . free.

And then her shoulders were pulling in, and her arms were becoming more sinewy. Her fingers were retracting, but in their place long, curved claws were extending. Her legs were twisting, the joints changing. And from the sensitive place at the end of her spine, the place that always felt unfinished when she was in human form, something long and flexible was springing. It lashed behind her with fierce joy.

Her jumpsuit was gone. The reason was simple: she wore only clothes made out of the hair of other shapeshifters. Even her boots were made of the hide of a dead shifter. Now both were being replaced by her own fur, thick black velvet with darker black rosettes. She felt complete and whole in it.

Her arms—now her front legs—dropped to the ground, her paws hitting with a soft but heavy thump. Her face prickled with sensitivity; there were long, slender whiskers extending from her cheeks. Her tufted ears twitched alertly.

A rasping growl rose in her chest, trying to escape from her throat. She held it back—that was easy and instinctive. A panther was by nature the best stalker in the world.

The next thing she did was instinctive, too. She took a moment to gauge the distance from herself to the black-haired boy. She took a step or two forward, her shoulders low. And then she jumped.

Swift. Supple. Silent. Her body was in motion. It was a high, bounding leap designed to take a victim without an instant of warning. She landed on the dark boy's back, clinging with razor claws.

Her jaws clamped on the back of his neck. It was the way panthers killed, by biting through the spine.

The boy yelled in rage and pain, grabbing at her as her weight knocked him to the ground. It didn't do any good. Her claws were too deep in his flesh to be shaken off, and her jaws were tightening with bone-crushing pressure. A little blood spilled into her mouth, and she licked it up automatically with a rough, pointed tongue.

More yelling. She was dimly aware that the vampires were attacking her, trying to wrench her away, and that the security guards were yelling. She ignored it all. Nothing mattered but taking the life under her claws.

She heard a sudden rumble from the body beneath her. It was lower in pitch than anything human ears could pick up, but to Keller it was both soft and frighteningly loud.

Then the world exploded in agony.

The dragon had caught hold of her fur just above the right shoulder. Dark energy was crackling into her, searing her. It was the same black power he'd used against Winnie, except that now he had direct contact.

The pain was scalding, nauseating. Every nerve ending in Keller's body seemed to be on fire, and her shoulder was a solid red blaze. It made her muscles convulse involuntarily and spread a metallic taste through her mouth, but it didn't make her let go. She held on grimly, letting the waves of energy roll through her, trying to detach her mind from the pain.

What was frightening was not just the power but the sense of the dragon's mind beneath it. Keller could feel a terrible coldness. A core of mindless hatred and evil that seemed to reach back into the mists of time. This creature was old. And although Keller couldn't tell what he wanted with the present age, she knew what he was focused on right now.

Killing her. That was all he cared about.

And of course he was going to succeed. Keller had known that from the beginning.

But not before I kill you, she thought.

She had to hurry, though. There almost certainly were other Night People in the mall. These guys could call for reinforcements, and they would probably get them.

You can't . . . make me . . . let go, she thought.

She was fighting to close her jaws. He was much tougher than a normal human. Panther jaws could crush the skull of a young buffalo. And right now, she could hear muscle crunching, but still she couldn't finish him.

Hang on . . . hang on . . .

Black pain . . . blinding . . .

She was losing consciousness.

For Winnie, she thought.

Sudden strength filled her. The pain didn't matter anymore. She tossed her head, trying to break his neck, wrenching it back and forth.

The body underneath her convulsed violently. She could

feel the little lapsing in it, the weakening that meant death was close. Keller felt a surge of fierce joy.

And then she was aware of something else. Someone was pulling her off the dragon. Not in the fumbling way the thugs had. This person was doing it skillfully, touching pressure points to make her claws retract, even getting a finger into her mouth, under the short front teeth between the lethal canines.

No! Keller thought. From her panther throat came a short, choking snarl. She lashed out with her back legs, trying to rip the person's guts out.

No. The voice didn't come in through Keller's ears. It was in her mind. A boy's voice. And it wasn't afraid, despite the fact that she was now scrabbling weakly, still trying to turn his stomach to spaghetti. It was concerned and anxious but not afraid. *Please—you have to let go.*

Even as he said it, he was pushing more pressure points. Keller was already weak. Now, all at once, she saw stars. She felt her hold on the dragon loosen.

And then she was being jerked backward, and she was falling. A hundred and ten pounds of black panther was landing on whoever had yanked her free.

Dizzy . . .

Her vision was blurred, and her body felt like rubber. She hardly had enough strength to twist her head toward the boy who had pulled her away.

Who was he? *Who?*